THE COMPOUND

S. A. BODEEN

FEIWEL AND FRIENDS

NEW YORK

For Bailey

A FEIWEL AND FRIENDS BOOK
An Imprint of Macmillan

THE COMPOUND. Copyright © 2008 by S. A. Bodeen. All rights reserved.
Printed in the United States of America. For information, address
Feiwel and Friends, 175 Fifth Avenue, New York, N.Y. 10010.

Library of Congress Cataloging-in-Publication Data

Bodeen, S.A. (Stephanie A.),
The compound / S. A. Bodeen.—p. cm.
ISBN-13: 978-0-312-57539-7   ISBN-10: 0-312-57539-4
[1. Survival—Fiction.   2. Deception—Fiction.   3. Psychopaths—Fiction.
4. Twins—Fiction.   5. Fathers—Fiction.] I. Title.
PZ7.B63515Co 2008
[Fic]—dc22
2007036148

First Edition: May 2008

Feiwel and Friends logo designed by Filomena Tuosto

10 9 8 7 6 5 4 3 2 1

www.feiwelandfriends.com

This is the way the world ends
This is the way the world ends
This is the way the world ends
Not with a bang but a whimper.

—T. S. ELIOT

PROLOGUE

T. S. ELIOT WAS WRONG. MY WORLD ENDED WITH A BANG the minute we entered the Compound and that silver door closed behind us.

The sound was brutal.

Final.

An echoing, resounding boom that slashed my nine-year-old heart in two. My fists beat on the door. I bawled. The screaming left me hoarse and my feet hurt.

Through my tears, the bear and elk on my father's shirt swam together. Beneath the chamois, Dad's chest heaved. The previous forty minutes had left us out of breath. Finally my gaze focused and went beyond him, searching. I gulped down a painful sob.

Had everyone made it?

Farther down the corridor I saw my weeping mother, dressed in a burgundy robe, dark tendrils dangling from her once-careful braid. Mom clutched my six-year-old sister,

Terese, a sobbing pigtailed lump in pink flowered flannel. From one small hand dangled her beloved Winnie the Pooh.

Behind them stomped my eleven-year-old sister, Lexie, dark hair mussed, arms crossed over the front of her blue silk pajamas. Not being brother-of-the-year material, I almost didn't care if she made it or not.

But my grandmother wasn't in sight.

"Where's Gram?" I shouted.

Dad patted my head, hard and steady, like I was a dog. He spoke slowly, in the same tone he used to explain to the household help the exact amount of starch he required in his shirts. "Eli, listen to me. There wasn't enough time. I waited as long as I could. It was imperative I get the rest of you to safety. We had to shut the door before it was too late."

The door. Always, the door.

Another look. No sign of my twin brother. He was the person I needed the most. Where was he?

My pounding heart suggested I already knew the answer. "Eddy?" His name caught in my throat, stuck tight by the panic rising up from my belly.

Dad whirled around, his tone accusing. "I thought Eddy was with you."

My head swung from side to side. Between sobs, the words barely eked out. "He went with Gram."

Dad's face clouded with indecision. Just for a moment. Had that moment lasted, it might have changed all of our futures. But Dad snapped back into control. "I still have one of you." With just six words, my childhood ended.

As did the rest of the world.

I knew what happened that night. We had been prepared. Other kids got bedtime stories about fairies and dogs. We fell asleep with visions of weapons of mass destruction dancing in our heads. Every evening, dinner included updates Dad downloaded from the Internet, updates on the U.S. involvement in the Middle East, the status of nuclear weapons programs in places like Iran and North Korea, names of countries that had been added to the list of those with WMDs.

Dad gripped my shoulders and pulled me away from the silver door, twisting me around to follow the rest of my family. What was left of it. I clung to my father's hand. He rushed ahead of me, his hand dropping mine.

I lifted my hand to my face and it reeked of fuel.

The corridor ended. We paraded through an archway strung with twinkling white lights, then entered an enormous circular room. The place reminded me of a yurt we'd built in school, only about eighty times bigger. The curved walls were made of log beams; the same type that crisscrossed over our heads in an intricate pattern. The roundness of the room was odd yet comforting.

Unlit logs sat in an elaborate stone fireplace, around which luxurious, overstuffed couches, love seats, and armchairs formed an audience. For a few seconds, despite the situation, my nine-year-old mind pondered what wonderful forts could be made with all those cushions.

Mom sat on a green couch and cradled Terese, while Lexie stood beside them, glowering. Dad lit kindling between the logs in the fireplace. The familiar smell of

3

wood smoke wafted toward us, seeming out of place in a setting so distinctly unfamiliar. My father put his hand on my mother's shoulder. His knuckles were white. He chose that moment to tell my mother and sisters that Gram and Eddy hadn't made it.

The announcement made it real. Made it final. A verbal execution.

Wails erupted from inside me. Mom and Lexie cried, too.

I ran to my mother. She held me along with Terese. Lexie leaned against Dad, and his arms encircled her.

We stayed that way for a long time, my face crushed to Mom's bosom. She smelled of lilacs. As I sobbed, she stroked my hair. Like always, Mom's touch was comforting and warm. Even that night, that heinous night, her touch helped. Our cries sounded over the crackling of the logs. After a long while, sobs faded to sniffs and shudders, waning from fresh grief into leftovers.

Feeling the need to move, I stood up. I wiped my nose with my sleeve, and climbed onto a stool by a large bar with a stainless steel refrigerator behind it.

Dad flicked a switch.

A plasma television dropped down from the ceiling, blank monitor glowing. "I figured we'd be in here a lot." The blue from the television tinted Dad's face and blond hair in a garish way. He startled me when he threw his arms out to the side. "Cozy, yes? What do you think?"

"It's not what I expected." Mom's voice was shaky.

Dad rubbed his jaw. "What did you expect?"

I had a pretty good idea what Mom was thinking. In

third grade, I gave an oral report on nuclear war. If you lived in a target area like we did, you had approximately forty minutes after nuclear weapons were launched. Forty minutes to do what? Say good-bye to loved ones, stuff yourself with doughnuts, take a hundred-mile-an-hour joy ride: whatever one did with only forty minutes left to live.

If you were me, the son of Rex Yanakakis, billionaire? Those forty minutes were spent escaping to an underground shelter, built specifically for the Yanakakis family. Here, I would live out the next fifteen years in luxurious comfort while nearly everyone else perished. We hadn't seen the shelter, only heard Dad talk about it. So I think Mom felt like I did, a little surprised the place actually existed.

"I don't know." Mom's head swayed slightly. The movement caused a tear to drip off the slope of her nose. "At least it's quiet down here."

Dad observed her for a moment. Then he switched off the television. "Eli? Lexie? Want to see your rooms?"

Our grave circumstances had not yet sunk in. I was a robot, dazed, simply sliding off the stool to follow my father and my older sister. It felt like a dream. Through a doorway on the opposite side of the room from where we'd entered, we proceeded down a long carpeted hallway similar to the ones in our house in Seattle. Only difference was this one smelled of vanilla and had the constant hum of a generator.

Dad narrated as we walked. "All the walls are reinforced, as we discussed, to keep out radiation. But the concrete is not pleasant to look at, so all the rooms are finished

5

in wallboard or wood. I didn't want you to feel surrounded by concrete and steel."

Dad stopped in front of a purple door. Lexie pushed it open and squealed. Leave it to her to cheer up over material possessions. Like something out of an Arabian Nights book, silk tapestries and curtains of bright colors were draped everywhere. A monstrous canopy bed ran the length of one whole wall. There was an exotic, cloying aroma. Incense maybe?

Lexie disappeared into the closet. When Dad talked about the Compound, he told us we'd have duplicates of everything we treasured. What an idiot I had been, to believe everything I cherished could be reproduced.

We left Lexie to explore and continued down the corridor. Dad indicated my room on the right. I pushed open the red door. Fresh-smelling meadowy air blew softly into my face. A bed took up the entire near wall, but there was no canopy like Lexie's. Instead, I looked up at the night sky.

Dad's hand squeezed my shoulder. "The constellations rotate. It's timed to be accurate from sundown to sunup, and will alter with the seasons. You can even choose the southern hemisphere if you like. During the day the bulbs mimic the actual progression of the sun. Of course, you have artificial light available at any time, but I thought you might miss your sunsets."

My sunsets? Not just mine. I wanted to shout at him. They were Eddy's sunsets, too.

Every day since we were seven, Eddy and I sat on the front lawn of our estate and watched the sun set over Puget

Sound. The evening ritual began with Els, an old lady from Belgium, who was one of our family's cooks. Hardly taller than Eddy and me, she wore her silver hair in a bun and squeaked around in white orthopedic shoes. As a rule, she never smiled.

One evening after dinner, she set out ice cream and bowls for sundaes, then left us to make our own. Sometimes we'd make a little mess, usually just drippings on the counter, smears of chocolate sauce. But that day I dropped a scoop of ice cream on the red-tiled counter. Instead of just picking it up, I poured fudge sauce over it. Eddy giggled and squirted whipped cream on top. I added a few cherries. We laughed. Then we filled our dishes.

Before we were done, Els returned. She saw the chaos and must have known I had caused it. She shook her finger in my face, speaking in her strong accent: "Brat, you are always a brat." She grabbed me by one ear. Her pinching grip was extra firm. From decades of kneading, I imagined. She had no trouble dragging me out the door.

I fell to my knees on the soft lawn. My ear hurt and I rubbed it while scowling up at her. "I'm telling my dad!"

Els raised her hands. "What will he say? He tells you always, 'Go out, get fresh air.' I give you fresh air." She slammed the door.

Eddy had followed us outside with an ice cream sundae in each hand, splotches of whipped cream adorning his face. He sat down next to me and handed me a bowl. Banished to the lawn, we ate our ice cream and perceived the sunset as an actual event for the first time ever. The next

7

day, we found ourselves waiting for it to happen again.

Sunsets, imitation or not, would no longer be the same.

Still, knowing my dad expected it of me, I lamely thanked him for the extravagant special effects. The room was done in the primary colors that appeal to boys of nine. One wall held shelves that stretched into the stars, and a speedy scan revealed my favorite books and other possessions. Copies, of course.

Dad asked me if I wanted to see more of the Compound.

I didn't. We would have to wait fifteen years, fifteen years before it would be safe to go outside. Which left more than enough time to see the rest of the Compound. Our new world. A new world I would soon hate.

Dad rubbed my shoulder. Suddenly his touch suffocated me. My stomach lurched, and I thought I might be sick. I wriggled down, away from his grip.

We went back to the family room. Terese slept on the couch. When Mom saw us, she shifted Terese off her lap and stood. Her eyes were vacant as she went behind the bar and made instant hot chocolate with marshmallows in the microwave.

I don't recall finishing my drink. I just remember feeling the emptiness in my gut. And the guilt. Nothing would ever be the same without Eddy, but I had to live with that. Why? Because it was my fault he wasn't there. My fault Eddy was dead. That night, I blamed myself.

Almost six years later, the feeling was just as strong. As was the feeling that all was not right in our new world.

CHAPTER ONE

Terese dribbled past me, switching hands as I'd taught her. A few months shy of twelve, she'd gotten taller in the last year, but still came only halfway up my chest. With her dark hair in the same braids she always had, the shrimp looked closer to ten.

Mom, Lexie, and Terese had white T-shirts and velour jogging suits in every color that particular clothing company produced. Even though Terese had plenty to choose from, she always wore purple.

Little Miss Perfect annoyed me, the way she always seemed so hell-bent on doing the right thing. Fluent in French, she also played the oboe. Hers was custom-made of the best grenadilla, African black wood. Dad brought it home from Paris when Terese was five. What other kid that age had a $10,000 oboe? I suppose I couldn't talk. Dad bought my $4,000 Getzen trumpet when I was six.

But down here my choices of people to hang out with were limited. Time wasn't.

Almost six years in the Compound.

Six years.

Well over two thousand days, most of them pretty much the same. But routine tends to equal comfort, which does provide some semblance of security. My alarm went off at seven. I rose to do tai chi for a half hour. Gram had taught Eddy and me the summers we stayed with her in Hawaii. The exercise ritual made me feel closer to both of them.

Then I showered. The bathroom was dark blue marble, with a huge whirlpool tub as well as a step-in shower that could hold an entire football team. A mirror ran the length of the room and I had two sinks all to myself. I switched every other day, with no particular reason why. Guess I relished having an option. Not a lot of those underground.

Most days, I weighed myself and checked out my body in the mirror. I was six feet and still growing, one hundred eighty pounds, and my muscles were well defined. Was I vain? I don't think so. I worked hard at getting my physique to that level. The outside was a lot easier to perfect than the inside.

For obvious reasons, thoughts of Eddy invaded me most when I looked in the mirror. If he were alive, I wondered, would he have had the same build? Same hair? Looking to control some aspect of my life, I'd refused to cut my hair after I turned twelve . It fell past my shoulders. Sometimes I left it down, so I had to peer out from behind a curtain. I couldn't see anyone. Made me believe they couldn't see me either.

I pulled my hair back into a ponytail secured with bands I'd taken from Lexie. It was nice, having the same face as Eddy. I never had to struggle to picture him; I simply looked in the mirror. Some days that face was a comfort. But other days, I couldn't bear to see his face—or mine.

Every day, I dressed in jeans and a T-shirt emblazoned with Dad's company's logo, YK, the biggest computer manufacturer and software developer in the world. Early on in the Compound, Dad explained there was clothing in every size we might possibly need.

He just neglected to mention that while sizes were limitless, style selection was not. In addition to jeans and YK T-shirts, my wardrobe consisted of gray sweatpants. Certainly didn't take me long to pick something out in the morning.

In our old world, my favorite shirt was an orange-and-white-striped rugby. Eddy had one, too, but he never wore his. I loved orange so much that I practically wore out that shirt. When we arrived down here, there was one in my closet, but I outgrew it. After I told Mom it was too small, it just didn't come back from the laundry. I missed the color. If I could have had one new thing to wear, it would've been a big orange hooded sweatshirt.

My routine also included running six miles on the treadmill in the gym each afternoon. The gym was big, the type you'd see in a school or YMCA, with an extra fifty feet or so at the end for fitness machines. A rower, an elliptical machine, a treadmill, and a recumbent bike made up the cardio part, with a boatload of free weights for the strength portion. No one lifted weights except me anymore.

In the old world, and for a time in the new, Dad was obsessive about exercise. He was obsessive about a lot of things, but exercise was near the top. He told me that a powerful man should have a powerful body as well. He's the one who got me into lifting and running every day. So I was surprised when he just stopped. It wasn't a gradual thing, where he'd just skip a day and then start up again. One day he just stopped and I never saw him set foot in the gym again. I didn't ask why. I never asked why. We weren't allowed to question our father in the old world, and the same rule applied in the Compound. Anyway, nothing he could say would change our reality.

Besides, I liked having the place to myself. Most of the time. Mom used the cardio equipment when she felt up to it. And once in a while I'd break routine and shoot baskets with Terese.

I lunged, stealing the ball from her a bit too rough. I was careful not to let my hands touch her. Since that first night in the Compound I didn't ever touch anyone with my bare hands. "You have to protect it, Reese."

Terese stopped to look at me, her green eyes bright. "I have been thinking about Father."

As much as I heard my sister speak every day, I could never get used to that English accent. Or the way she called our parents Mother and Father. Like all of us, she had her own routines, one of which was to watch *Mary Poppins* at least once a day. She must have seen it more than a thousand times. I wished that DVD would finally wear out.

She sucked on one of her braids. "Do you hate him?"

I shot and missed.

Her eyebrows went up. "I just wondered."

The ball bounced off the wall and rolled back toward me. I retrieved it and dribbled. I ignored her, figuring she'd keep talking anyway. It was nothing new, for her to talk about Dad behind his back, then be all adoring daughter to his face.

She kept on talking. "I do, you see. I think I might hate him." She caught my pass and did a layup.

I shook my head, rebounded, shot again, then caught the ball when it dropped through the net.

Granted, I wasn't Dad's biggest fan. He ran our lives in the Compound the way he had on the outside. The only one who had ever questioned Dad's decisions was Gram. She was the one person I'd seen stand up to him. The last time Eddy and I went to Hawaii with her, we almost didn't get to go. And I wanted to go so badly. She lived in a small rural community, all locals descended from long lines of locals, where no one cared who we were. For those short weeks we spent with her every summer, we were just kids from the mainland.

At first, Dad refused. He said we should be at home going to science and math camps. But Gram marched into his office, dressed in a hibiscus-covered muumuu. She emerged a few minutes later, wide smile on her face. Dad had been close behind, a frown on his.

I could only imagine how different things would be in the Compound if Gram had made it.

For the rest of us, challenging Dad's judgment was out of the question. And I'd stopped asking him the first year whether he'd been able to make contact with anyone on the outside, and how long our supplies of water, food, and power would last. "I've planned for every contingency" was his stock reply.

And there was the way he would spend a week in bed, then all of a sudden not sleep for days. Weird. Even then, we never voiced our doubts about his leadership.

Besides, would it have changed our situation? Made things better?

No.

So there was no point. We all knew it.

Terese bent down to tie one of her shoes. They were the same white top-of-the-line cross trainers that we all wore, which lay stacked in boxes in every size in one of the storerooms. "I believe I do hate Father. He did this to us; he made me leave my friends and my school. He makes us stay here."

Usually I just let her motormouth wear itself out, but I was in an ornery mood. "That's pretty stupid." I tossed the ball from one hand to the other. "If we weren't here, do you know where we'd be?"

"Of course I do." Terese straightened back up. "We would be home in Seattle with Eddy and Clementine."

Until that moment, I'd forgotten about Clementine, Terese's rag doll kitten. Clementine was cute, acted more like a dog than a cat. As allergic as he was, even Eddy played with Clementine until he wheezed.

"Eli, you'd be there with Cocoa." Her tone was nanny-ish and condescending.

Just the mention of Cocoa's name stopped my breath for a minute. My chocolate lab puppy, a constant fixture on my bed and at my side. I missed her. But I pushed away the memories. "You're being ridiculous. No one is there anymore. You know about the bombs, right?"

"Eli." Her voice got louder, but she was still matter-of-fact. "Perhaps we could find someone, perhaps others are alive. I hate Father for doing this to us."

I rolled my eyes and listened to the rant. Little Miss Perfect was losing it. I knew what the whole situation had done to me when I was nine, I couldn't imagine what adverse effects it had had on an almost six-year-old's mental state. (Actually I could, given the whole Mary Poppins thing.) Making up a scenario you could live with was easier than dealing with a reality you could not. I understood the benefits of that.

"Okay," I said.

Her eyebrows went up in sync with the corners of her mouth. "So you do believe me?"

"Of course." Among other talents, I had always been a decent liar.

Terese's shoulders drooped. "I miss home dreadfully. I wish we were there with Gram and Eddy."

"Yeah, well, wish in one hand, crap in the other, and see which fills up first." I'd also always been a stellar jerk.

"Grow the hell up. Eddy's dead. Gram's dead. They're gone. Forever. Deal with it."

My sister's mouth dropped open, and then slowly closed. Her eyes narrowed. "You're not at all like Eddy."

It was definitely time for her to leave. My toes lined up slightly behind the free-throw line. Every day I shot three hundred of them. I started shooting them the first full day here. After six years, my percentage had improved to eighty-four. "You don't even remember Eddy. You were too young."

"I do so remember him." She tilted her head a bit, studying me. "He looked like you."

My follow-through was practiced and precise. "That's a little easy, don't you think?" *Swoosh.* "You see me every day."

Her hands were on her hips. "He wasn't at all mean like you. He was nice. And he cared more about stuff."

My first thought was to protest, but I realized it wasn't worth the breath. She was right. I got the rebound and lined up again. Tried to concentrate. Pretended she was a jeering crowd. It wasn't much of a stretch.

Terese continued to pounce. "At least he played with me. You never did. You always ignored me. You even teased him for playing with me; you said I was a baby."

There wasn't much to say in my defense. In the old world, Eddy and I were so close that I never made a point of reaching out to our sisters. The reason was simple: I didn't need them. Between school, ballet, and piano, Lexie wasn't around that much, but Terese was. Eddy always saved time for her.

The ball left my hands. The shot was good.

Terese kept up her rant. "You ignored me in here until I was ten." Her face was red, but I knew she wouldn't cry. Early on she learned, as we all did, that tears didn't help. They wouldn't bring back anything or anyone.

She held up four fingers as I jogged after the ball. "Four years, Eli. Four years you didn't even look at me."

There was a good reason for that. She reminded me too much of Eddy, the way he was kind to everyone, same as my mom. Part of me hated Terese for being so good, for being the one everyone adored.

It made me miss him more.

Despite the fact that I tended to treat Terese badly, she kept coming back for more. Maybe because I was as close as she was ever going to get to Eddy. Even so, I knew where she was coming from, missing Eddy like she did. I was sure she'd rather have him instead of me. Eddy was the kind of older brother anyone would want. He had always been the kind of brother I wanted. For nine years, he'd been the kind of brother I had. But I had screwed that up in a big way.

I chucked the ball at my sister, hard, smacking her on the butt.

"Ow!" She scowled.

I laughed.

"You're so mean." Her accent wavered when she got ticked off. She grabbed her ratty old Pooh from his spot by the door and left.

Alone at last.

But as I shot my free throws, I couldn't stop thinking about what my sister had said. Stupid kid could make up stories. It was definitely a coping mechanism. But my gut was wrenched. Was it the mention of Eddy? Or the fact that someone besides me admitted they thought about him on a regular basis? Even though it was just Little Miss Perfect, someone besides me believed maybe he was out there somewhere. Alive. I tried so hard *not* to think of him. *Not* to believe he might have survived.

People often talk about uncanny connections between identical twins. About twins raised separately who end up innately similar. That wasn't the case with Eddy and me, as we were always together, everything in our environment the same. We took our first steps the same day. Lost our first baby teeth within hours of each other. Both grew two inches in the same summer.

And we had our roles.

He was the leader. I let him lead, because I liked to follow. Followers were rarely accountable for their actions. In addition to leading, Eddy was also my protector. Always had been.

We were eight years old the last summer we stayed with Gram in Hawaii. One afternoon, we picnicked by a waterfall. Eddy and I lived in board shorts and rash guards that summer. Gram, smelling of White Shoulders, wore a red muumuu, her long hair loose, a pink pua flower behind one ear. She spread a dolphin print beach towel on the grass before laying out an appetizing buffet of Spam and rice, leftover kalua pork, Eddy's daily ration of Jack Link's beef jerky, which he couldn't live without, fresh mangoes, and guava juice. For dessert a small cooler held my favorite strawberry mochi ice cream balls.

We finished lunch. Eddy and I took a Frisbee and went off by ourselves. I followed Eddy up a steep hill and tossed the disk to him. The breeze from the falls pushed it back my way. I grabbed for it and missed, reaching so far that I lost my balance. As I tumbled down the hill, my back slammed into a tree. It stopped my downward progress, knocking away my breath. Arms waving, legs kicking, I struggled for air.

Eddy stood at the top of the hill. Over the rushing water he called to me, "Eli! Stop. Stop moving."

Minutes passed. My breath came back. I moved to get back up on my feet.

Again, Eddy called to me, "Eli, don't move. I'm coming."

Like a crab, he inched his way down the hill. As he came closer, his eyes narrowed at something past me. I twisted my head in order to see what he saw. The tree that had taken my breath was the only thing between me and the long, fatal drop to the rocks beneath the falls. I reached out for my brother.

Eddy pressed both his palms into my chest to calm me. "Eli, I got you, I got you." He gripped my arm and we crawled up the hill together.

At the top, relieved, I rolled over onto my back, panting. "Don't tell Gram."

Eddy was also winded. "Duh."

☢

BEING IN THE COMPOUND WITHOUT EDDY SEEMED TO GET harder every day. We didn't talk about him much. Dad had said early on that this was our life and we should move on, not keep thinking about the way things used to be. After talking to Terese that morning in the gym, remembering Eddy, all I wanted was to talk to him and pretend he could hear me. I tried to imagine our lives as they might have been. Sort of a What Would Eddy Do?

If things were normal and we were in the old world, going to high school, Eddy would probably have a million girlfriends. He'd had all the friends in grade school and I knew I was in the mix only because of him; high school wouldn't have been much different. I'd be getting dragged out on double dates with his girlfriends' friends. Knowing Eddy, he would probably insist on it.

Sometimes my thoughts took a different direction: What Would Eddy Do If Eddy Were Here?

I hit my fiftieth free throw.

Despite knowing he and Gram had perished on the outside that night six years before, I never truly felt our connection break. There was emptiness, of course. Along with a huge feeling of loss. But that feeling of connection only a twin could understand? That I still had.

Lining up my next shot, I started to release the ball.

"That's off."

The voice startled me even as I tried not to show it, although my lousy shot was proof enough.

Dad walked out of the shadows underneath the basket as my air ball went past him. He let it bounce off the wall before catching it, then tossed the ball from one hand to the other. "You and Terese have a nice game?"

"Huh?" That caught me off guard. Had he heard our conversation? "Um, yeah. Her game needs work, though."

Dad chuckled a bit, then tossed me the ball. "She has a grand imagination, that one."

I nodded, unsure what to say.

Walking toward the door, away from me, he paused but didn't turn around. "I'm sure you can set her straight."

"Set her straight?"

"Basketball." One hand raised in the air, the wrist flipped a bit. "Her game." And he left.

Although he didn't come out and say it, I sensed he had heard me and Terese. And after the exchange with my sister that morning in the gym, I wondered what Eddy *would* do if he were in the Compound instead of me. Despite believing I was dead, would he trust that feeling of connection and still hold out hope for a miracle?

Through 250 more free throws, of which I made 227, I already knew the answer. If there were even the slightest chance the world was not as it seemed, a tiny slice of hope that his twin might still be alive, he would find out. Or else die trying.

CHAPTER TWO

I WALKED INTO THE KITCHEN FOR DINNER, NOT EXPECTING to be greeted with rainbow-colored balloons and streamers. My family sat on the red leather banquettes in the breakfast nook, all eyes on me. Mom and Dad were on opposite sides, of course. As far away as they could get from each other while still putting on the illusion of a happy family.

Lexie was in her usual place, right at Dad's side. Maybe she thought she had a shot at becoming queen of the Compound. Her dark braid contrasted with the white of her T-shirt. She fixed me with a glare, even more piercing than usual.

Terese had a big smile on her face, definitely fake.

Mom's wasn't. Her dark hair was piled on her head and she wore red velour. Even a touch of red lipstick. Perhaps it was due to the occasion, but for whatever reason, she stood and her arms widened to give me a hug.

"Happy Birthday, Eli."

She noticed the dread in my face and the smile on hers wavered. She backed off.

No one touched me. No one ever touched me. I didn't allow them to. I didn't touch them either. Not since the night we arrived here.

I sat down on a stool by the granite counter away from everyone else.

Dad yawned. His hair was a blond helmet of bed head, and he wore his ancient bear and elk shirt. Arms crossed, hands spread out on his shoulders, he looked like he was chilly. "Your fifteenth birthday, son."

Not just my birthday. Eddy's, too. That's why I had been thinking of Eddy so much. My gut had realized it was our birthday even though my brain didn't. I didn't own a calendar. And I sure as hell didn't mark off the days like some survivor on a desert island. I pretty much just waited for Mom and Dad to announce the holidays, the only Compound days that differed from regular ones.

Most holidays in the Compound were a welcome departure from the routine. Even though we lived in a microcosm where things never strayed from the unremarkable, holidays still held some surprises. The day after Thanksgiving we put up an artificial tree and decorations, hung stockings by the fireplace in the family room. On December 25, we awoke at some ungodly hour by Terese's cheerful "Happy Christmas, everyone!"

Down in the family room, we found our bulging stockings. I admired Dad for managing to think of every detail.

There was always something to open. Terese would get a doll or toy she didn't already have. I'd get a video game. Lexie, some sheet music or ballet shoes. Although I knew where all the supplies were, Dad was able to keep a whole store of things secret, things he could bring out on birthdays and Christmas to make us feel like normal kids. And most of the time it worked. Even if it was just for one day.

My birthday wasn't something I wanted to be reminded of, let alone celebrate. July 16. Once we were in the Compound, I found it ironic that Eddy and I were born on that day, the umpteenth anniversary of the inaugural nuclear explosion at the Trinity test site. Most dads had hobbies that they passed down to their sons; hunting, fishing, auto repair. Dad's hobby was nuclear war, which meant his sons knew everything about it.

To Eddy and me, it was cool. War was exciting, especially nuclear war. But it was exciting in the same way a California earthquake might be exciting to a person from the Midwest, or a tornado might be exciting to someone who lives in New England, where they never occur. We thought it was something we would never experience, so we weren't afraid.

Those scientists didn't really know what they had created at first. Even their name for the atomic bomb was innocuous: the Gadget. But when they saw it brought to life, they realized soon enough. Oppenheimer himself later quoted some old text: "I am become death, the destroyer of worlds."

Yeah, they realized soon enough. They probably realized

weeks later on August 6, when the United States bombed Hiroshima, and then August 9, Nagasaki. The events of July 16 paled next to those.

July 16 wasn't just my birthday. It was also the anniversary of the day we entered the Compound. That terrible night when, because of me, Eddy was gone forever. If it were up to me, I would never acknowledge the date. Celebrating the worst day of my life was insane. But I think celebrating the day only as my birthday—nothing else—helped the rest of the family in some way.

Mom handed me a package. "It's from all of us."

My fingers tore away the wrinkled white tissue paper. A first edition of *On the Beach*, a 1950s classic about the world after a nuclear war. It would have been valuable if the real world still existed. Of course I'd read it before; there was a paperback copy in the library.

I forced myself to look pleased as I opened the cover.

Dad had written the inscription, dated of course. Never without a black fine-point Sharpie, he always dated everything. In the old world, he dated boxes of cereal when the groceries were delivered. He dated packages that arrived in the mail. Whenever we went through the Starbucks drive-through to get his coffee, he'd date the paper cup. I wouldn't be surprised if he'd Sharpied the date on my forehead when I was born.

I flipped the page.

Like the first time I'd seen them, T. S. Eliot's cruel words struck me. That was the only passage I would ever read of this edition. Of course I would set it among the others on a shelf in my room, but it was a work I never wanted to read again. The survivors in the book stirred up jealousy in me. They saw the end creeping toward them, but all the while they were still in control of their own destiny. Yes, they were doomed, but they had the opportunity to choose when their final breaths occurred.

I envied them that, having cyanide as an option. Not that I would have chosen death over life in the Compound. But at least they had a tangible choice. I didn't.

I felt Dad watching me so I forced a smile as I shut the book and thanked everyone. Then we had dinner, spinach salad alongside vegetarian lasagna with fresh peppers and tomatoes from hydroponics. The noodles were in pieces, they were so old, but it still tasted good. I didn't look forward to birthday cake because there wouldn't be any. We no longer had all the ingredients.

That had come to light a few weeks before. I had been in the kitchen, doing Mandarin vocabulary at the booth.

Mom was at the espresso machine, making her third Americano of the morning. For her, Dad had stockpiled what must have been tons of Tully's whole bean French roast coffee. Decaf.

I was on my first, and only, of the day.

She took a sip out of her green-plaid insulated mug. "Eli, I want to show you something." Still holding her cup of non-caffeine, Mom stood at the door to the pantry and beckoned. Inside, she pointed out a sack of flour. "Look in that."

The burlap was folded open. The grayish flour stuck to my fingers. "I thought flour didn't go bad."

She took a drink. "I thought so, too. I'm wondering if it's not entirely wheat. Maybe something else got mixed in."

I held my hand to my nose and sniffed. Didn't smell right. Didn't smell *that* bad, though. "Is it all like this?"

"I don't know." She twisted a bit of her hair. "I don't want you or the girls to eat any of it."

I looked at her. "You're not going to get rid of it?"

She bit the inside of her lip. "You know how your father likes bread."

My eyes widened. "You've been feeding him bread from this?"

She nodded. "I mean, not yet. I just found this today. If he gets sick, then I'll stop. I just . . . I just don't want to give him any indication the food situation has worsened."

That surprised me, coming from her. "Why not?"

She looked straight at me, almost like it was a challenge. "I just don't. So I'm going to keep on like everything is fine. But I don't want you or the girls to eat any bread I make."

I knew she wouldn't take the chance of using that flour to make cake, even for my birthday.

Back in my room, I treated myself to a Snickers from the stale stash under my bed. In honor of my Super-Duper Special Day. As I chewed, I couldn't help but remember other birthdays. The ones in the Compound blended together, not worth reminiscing about.

But the ones on the outside? They were dream parties, fantasies befitting the twin sons of a billionaire.

Pony rides and moonwalks and huge theme cakes and,

for our eighth birthday, a clown show plus players from the Seahawks. I thought we were too old for the clown. But that was the part of the party Dad let Mom plan, so Eddy persuaded me not to make a fuss.

That year should have been the best. Every boy from our class was invited, of course. But I knew they came for Eddy, not me. Eddy was kind to everyone, fun to be with, popular. I was just his twin; not so kind, not so fun. Definitely not popular. As Eddy's twin, I was tolerated. We were a package—buy one, get one.

We were all outside. The front lawn had been transformed into a football field by temporary white chalk lines. The Seahawks played flag football with us for a long time. I should have been enjoying it.

I wasn't.

I'd seen the boys from our class arrive, all bearing gifts. Of course they each brought two, one for me, one for Eddy. I could tell some were the same, but lots of them were different. Eddy's presents were probably something cool. Mine? Not so much. I suppose it showed the degree to which we were liked. Or as in my case, not liked.

The blatant disparity bothered me. So I decided to do something about it.

With everyone out on the front lawn, I claimed I had to use the bathroom. I darted into the house, stopping to grab a roll of tape. In the backyard, a white tent was set up for the cake and presents and the clown show. At the table of gifts, I started switching tags. All the labels with Eddy's name went on the presents for me, and vice versa.

My movements were hurried as I tried to finish before anyone came.

"Hey, kid!"

I jumped, startled, and the tape dropped from my hand.

The hired clown, in his white face, red nose, goofy striped outfit, and yellow clown shoes, stood there watching me. "What are you doing?"

Words didn't come. What was I supposed to say? Laughter and cheers came toward us. I kicked the roll of tape under the table and crossed my arms in defiance. What was the stupid clown going to do? Screw up his biggest payday of the year?

The kids poured in and the clown just raised his freakish eyebrows. "You're obviously the evil twin." He stepped up onstage to get ready for his show.

We opened presents. I saw the confused looks. Our guests wondered why I ended up with the better presents meant for Eddy. Maybe some would mention it to their mothers later, although with the excitement of the day most of them probably forgot.

And Eddy didn't know. Not only that, he didn't even notice what I opened, or compare his gifts to mine. He opened each one, making a big deal over it and the person who brought it. Somehow, he made each kid feel that he had given him the one thing he'd always wanted. Me? I remember ripping open one after the other. Maybe I thanked kids. Maybe I didn't. The presents were all dumb, anyway. I knew the good ones were yet to come.

That year Dad gave us laptops. Expensive prototypes not yet available on the market. Mine was exactly the same as Eddy's, like everything Dad gave us. He presented them to us in front of all the kids from school. They immediately crowded around Eddy, clamoring to see.

Left on the outside of the circle, I tucked the laptop under my arm and sat down to have some more cake. The clown was on his way out and stopped for a second. "Hope you got what you wanted, kid." He winked.

Yeah, there were a lot of reasons for me to forget that July 16 even existed. And even a few reasons to hate clowns.

☢

THINKING ABOUT OTHER BIRTHDAYS MADE ME UNCOMFORTABLE. I didn't feel like sitting in my room that whole night, thinking about the past. But I also didn't feel like hanging out with the family. Not that I ever did. They were busy with their own routines.

We did eat dinner together most nights. But after that we went our separate ways. Dad usually went and worked in his office. Lexie retreated to her room or helped Mom with laundry or other chores like that. Terese usually joined them.

That was one thing to be thankful for. Dad believed things like laundry and ironing were strictly women's work. Fine with me.

I went to pick out a DVD in the media room. Our collection of movies and music was incomparable, as if Dad had sauntered into Blockbuster and Music World and demanded one of everything. On the shelves beside the media were comprehensive catalogs, a product of my father's fastidious nature, listing every item available. Even after six years, I still hadn't watched or listened to nearly half of what that room had to offer.

I chose *The Matrix*, even though it was old and I'd seen it about a hundred times. Sometimes after I watched it, I pretended the Compound was simply an alternate reality and I would wake up any day in a better place.

My mom liked old Cary Grant movies. Sometimes I watched with her. She had a great laugh, an infectious kind that made everyone laugh along. It seemed Cary Grant was the only person who could draw it out of her anymore.

In the family room, Lexie was already watching a movie on the big screen. Horror, of course. Her routine. Sometimes I watched them with her, but she creeped me out more than the movies did. Lexie sat on the couch, not moving, her long, dark hair masking her face. Even during parts that made me flinch or jump or look away, my sister just sat there. Staring. Why was it that nothing seemed to scare her?

I stood in front of her, blocking her view, forcing her to look somewhere other than the screen.

Lexie sighed and tucked her hair behind her ears, revealing her face. She was pretty, with hazel eyes that lit up when she smiled, which wasn't very often. "Move, stupid."

"I want to watch something else."

My sister finally looked directly at me, like I hadn't

existed before then. She frowned. "So, go watch it in your room."

"No. I want the big screen." I turned to the player and ejected her movie.

"Hey! I'm watching that."

"So." I inserted my DVD. "It's my birthday."

"Oh my God." She laughed and mimicked me. *"It's my birthday."* When she stood up, the top of her head was even with my chin. "I'm watching my movie." With one fuzzy-slippered foot, she tried to push me away.

I laughed. "Ooh, tough guy." She was strong but light, so it didn't take much effort on my part to shove her with one sock-covered foot.

As she fell back on the couch, she swiped at my face, barely missing it with her long, sharp, and perfectly shaped nails. Except for her left thumbnail, which she chewed incessantly.

Through the barrier of her blanket, I grabbed her arm and twisted it behind her back, forcing her face into the back of the couch. "Now I'm not positive, but I'm pretty sure I can take you."

Lexie tried to rip the blanket off me to get at my skin. To touch me, knowing full well my weakness. But I was stronger.

I smacked her face not all that lightly with her DVD, and then dropped it next to her. "So why don't you watch this in *your* room?" With an extra twist, I let go of her arm.

Lexie whirled around, pushing her hair away from her

reddening cheek. She picked up the disk. Before she left, she kicked me in the shin. "Happy frickin' Birthday."

I didn't bother to retaliate.

The Matrix came on. I dropped the blanket and sat down, rubbing my shin. *Yeah,* I thought. *Happy frickin' Birthday.*

CHAPTER THREE

IN HER OUTBURST ON MY BIRTHDAY, TERESE ACCUSED DAD of planning all of it. Of course he planned the Compound. We wouldn't still be alive if he hadn't. But she had made me think.

My father had given us a detailed orientation to the Compound when we first arrived. The structure was three stories underground, made mainly of concrete and steel. The operation of the Compound was fairly simple, as Dad explained it. Room temperature was kept at a constant seventy-two degrees, reverse osmosis technology made our water drinkable, and three industrial incinerators burned all the garbage and waste products, miles of ductwork taking the smoke far away from our pristine air supply.

The Compound itself must have taken years to build. I never asked for the details. It would be like a lion asking about who built his cage. Knowing more wouldn't make any of it easier.

But our birthday got me thinking about Eddy, about what he'd be like. Eddy would want to know everything about the Compound; he was always curious. Maybe that was a fault of mine—accepting things without ever questioning them. Or maybe I had just let him take care of that. But he wasn't around to take care of things anymore.

Across from my room was a blue door. Eddy's room. I had never been able to bring myself to enter. Besides, I assumed it was an exact copy of mine. I reached for the doorknob, but my hand hovered there, inches away, trembling a bit. Why did I feel the need to do this now? What good could it possibly do?

Maybe I was looking for a way to feel closer to Eddy. Maybe that's all it was.

With a deep breath, I twisted the knob and pushed.

The air smelled of oranges, almost too much so. I'd expected the room to smell musty, like a museum. I'd forgotten that it was connected to the same ventilation system as the rest of the Compound. The light switches were in the same spot as in my room. Nothing seemed to happen after I hit the first switch, but I soon saw that his ceiling was set to the sunrise. I turned it off and switched on the regular fluorescents.

I walked over to the bookshelves, ran my hands over a few of the books and toys. The bookshelves looked like mine used to; until I'd outgrown the books and toys and shoved everything in my closet. As I looked around that room, so much like mine had been, I felt strange, like I'd traveled back in time.

But something was missing. Dust. There was none.

I looked in the trash can. Several used dusting cloths lay inside. I leaned closer and sniffed. That was where the orange smell was coming from.

Except for the recent cleaning, it didn't look like anyone had stepped foot in there for a long time. If ever.

Inside the closet, I found nine-year-old Eddy's wardrobe on hangers; orderly, neat, and pressed. Never touched. I slammed the closet door, not wanting to see, not wanting to remember. As I backed away, my hip collided with the desk.

I shifted around. Something on the desk caught my eye. I grinned and reached out. A laptop. A duplicate of the ones we'd gotten at our clown and Seahawks birthday.

Whatever happened to mine?

I remembered.

Shortly after we entered the Compound, Dad had borrowed it, saying he wanted to upgrade it for me. Then he'd given me a different one, a better one. He said mine wasn't worth upgrading after all. I'd never asked for the first one back.

This laptop, the one intended for Eddy, was plugged in, the light proclaiming the battery to be charged. Had it been charging for six years? I opened it and hit the power button. As the icons appeared on the screen, my fingertips rested on one I hadn't seen for so long. Internet. That was the difference between this laptop and the one I used. Mine had no integrated wireless Internet.

My elbow rested on the desk and my head automatically

leaned on my palm. I stared at the screen. I hadn't forgotten about the Internet. I had just put it in the category of things I no longer had, things too painful to think about. Like Eddy.

Eddy and I had lived on the Internet, playing online games, instant messaging our friends. We even IM'ed each other at night, even though we were separated by only a bedroom wall.

My finger rubbed the cursor pad.

A message popped up on the screen.

Wireless Server Not Available.

Duh.

In that slim span of time, from the moment I'd powered up until that message appeared, I'd felt something. Was it hope? I hadn't felt hope for so long. Did I actually expect to be connected to the Internet? Maybe, somewhere in the back of my mind, I believed that one resourceful survivor had hooked it back up.

Yeah, right.

Dad told us early on that the Compound was wired for communication. At first, he checked daily for a signal, but his updates were always the same: Nothing. After a while, it was too depressing to ask. And he stopped mentioning it.

I maneuvered the cursor and clicked fast. The laptop hadn't yet been set up for Eddy. So I put in my own password, username, even entered my ID in the IM program. **TwinYan2.**

I smiled, imagining that **TwinYan1** was still out there,

just an IM away. I unhooked the power cord and wrapped it around my wrist.

"Eli?"

I jumped, and then felt stupid for being startled yet again.

Mom stood at the open door. "What are you doing in here?"

Did I even know? I shrugged. "I, uh . . . was missing Eddy. I've never been in here."

She nodded. "I don't think anyone has but me."

"You cleaned it?"

"Yes, I come in here now and then." She noticed the laptop in my hands. "What are you doing with that?"

"I was going to take it." I felt guilty.

Her eyes shifted, as if she was mulling something.

"I won't, though." I set the laptop back on the desk.

One hand covered her mouth for a moment. She started to shake her head, and then stopped. "No, take it."

"Are you sure?"

Mom nodded. "I kept it charged, I think." She never touched any computers. Maybe because it was Dad's thing. Maybe because she didn't like technology. She just didn't think they could add to her quality of life.

I said, "Yeah, it's charged."

"Just—"

"What?"

"Don't show it to your father, okay? He knows I come in here. That . . . it helps, somewhat. But I told him I'd leave everything as it was."

I picked up the laptop again. "I won't show anyone."

"Promise me you won't."

I promised. "Thanks, Mom."

My mother smiled. "And if there's anything else you want, go ahead. I don't think Eddy would mind." She straightened up. "Only keep it to yourself. Don't tell—"

"Who?"

"Never mind." She glanced around and left.

My eyes went to the closet door. Inside, I pawed through the hangers. Eddy's orange rugby was tucked between two sweaters. I pulled the shirt from the hanger and wrapped the laptop in it, then dropped the bundle off in my room. One day late, but hey. Happy Birthday to me.

I found myself grinning. What a great find. And in the first place I looked. Eddy would have been proud. I imagine he would have kept looking, to see what else he could uncover. Thinking about it spurred me on.

As I neared the family room, Dad's high-pitched cackle filled the air, which meant only one thing. He was watching a Woody Allen movie. I thought they were so stupid, but he would sit there for hours, laughing out loud. Maybe it was the combination of the two, Woody Allen's humor that I didn't get, along with my dad's bizarre laugh, but I just could not deal. I turned back the other way.

Down the hall, I came to Terese's room. I opened the door. It was still done up like the Hundred Acre Woods from Winnie the Pooh; her bed was still a giant honey pot. I suppose at the time he was building the Compound, my dad thought it was perfect. But she wasn't six anymore.

Dad had offered to paint it and put in a canopy bed from the storeroom. Terese refused, though, still climbing the little ladder into the honey pot every night.

I stepped closer to the bed and ran my hand over a ladder step. Dust came away on my fingers. I wiped it off on my shirt and walked over to the closet. Inside were dozens of empty hangers. A few clothes hung here and there, but it looked like she had moved out. I wondered what was up.

A ways down the hall was my parents' room. We weren't allowed in, although I'd caught a glance one time, and it looked to be an exact replica of the one in our mansion on Puget Sound. That one I had been in, plenty. When we were little, Mom had let us jump into bed with her after Dad went to work. He probably would have had a fit if he knew rowdy kids were eating their Cap'n Crunch on his expensive Egyptian linens.

The bedroom was decorated in wine and cream, with an oak king-size bed and matching armoires, dressers, and bureaus. Mom's favorite Monet hung on the wall over the headboard. It was the original, of course. I wondered if a replica hung on the wall of this bedroom.

Well, I wasn't going to snoop in there. Not yet, anyway.

I walked quickly past the next door, as I always did. I didn't want to acknowledge, let alone set eyes inside, that room. Knowing what was inside was bad enough. The door was painted a cheery yellow. Ironic.

The rooms went on and on, like berries on a bush. I stopped at the library, which held thousands of books in every possible genre: mystery, biography, historical, classics, legal thrillers, science fiction, and children's literature. Anything we might ever, or never, want to read.

Terese read every piece of British children's literature she could find. When she was younger, it had been *Paddington Bear* and *Winnie the Pooh*. Later it was *The Chronicles of Narnia* and everything by Roald Dahl. *Peter Pan* was her favorite.

Maybe that's why she still had her stuffed Winnie the Pooh and watched *Mary Poppins*. She saw the Compound as never-never land, a place where she would never have to grow up. Last time I'd seen her with a book, it had been *The Hobbit*, so maybe she finally decided to move on. For her sake, I hoped we had a lot of British stuff. I had even recommended some American authors to her, but she seemed stuck in her English fantasy.

A two-sided fireplace sat in the middle of the library, burnished leather armchairs facing it on either side. Cherry shelves stretched up to the top of the ceiling. Sliding ladders on each wall allowed us to reach everything.

Lexie read a lot of lengthy epic stories. She read *Cold Mountain* at least a dozen times. I finally got it away from her long enough to see what was so great about it. For a novel of the Civil War it was okay, but the ending was so depressing. I pegged Lexie as more of a fan of happy endings. But she still read it again and again. Maybe she was deluded enough to think the ending might change eventually. I gave up trying to figure it out.

My routine was to pick authors and read every book

they'd written. The entire previous spring I had spent many dreary hours with Dostoyevsky. I should have quit, but once I started something, I liked to finish. Stephen King was my current read. Living with anxiety and uncertainty (anxiety and uncertainty unrelated to my own circumstances) was invigorating. It was generous of Dad, I suppose, to furnish the place with so much stuff he would never read himself. He only read nonfiction, usually about wars or generals or politics.

I thought about stopping to read for a while, but I was too restless. I was ready to make another discovery, if there were any more to be made. And my gut said there were.

CHAPTER FOUR

I PASSED BY THE GYM. NO NEED TO SEE WHAT I ALREADY SAW every day. The restaurant-style kitchen was next. Stainless steel pots and pans in every size hung from the ceiling above a long butcher-block-style counter. Two ovens sat side by side on one wall. They were the Hansel and Gretel type, big enough to shove a good-size witch inside. Three stainless steel coolers with clear glass doors lined another wall. It seemed like overkill, to have such a massive kitchen for just our family. Not like we'd be throwing any parties.

The other end of the kitchen held the breakfast nook and the counter. Past them was the door into the dining room. One large crystal chandelier lit the room, which housed an oak dining table with seating for sixteen. Again, overkill. We ate Christmas, Thanksgiving, and Easter dinner in there. That was it.

I left the kitchen and headed to the infirmary. Although it was state of the art, it looked like an old-fashioned doctor's office, when the doctor had a small place and did everything in one room. It smelled like antiseptic, like a hospital. White cabinets with glass doors lined one wall, holding bandages, medicines, and other supplies. Two hospital beds were set up on one side. I pushed aside a curtain divider. Behind it were several machines. I knew the one was an EKG machine, but the rest I was unsure of. I assumed my dad had been trained on all of them at some point, otherwise why have them?

Every room in the Compound also held a defibrillator. It didn't make much sense to me. If one of us was going to check out, why not let us go? If we truly had a heart problem, there was no one to do surgery on us. What could a defibrillator buy us? A few minutes?

I looked over the medicine cabinet. It wasn't locked, despite having a lot of controlled substances inside. I don't know who, if anyone, ever took them. Dad told us never to touch any of them. That was all he had to do. The one quality the Yanakakis kids did have in common was obedience. I switched off the lights before I left.

The beauty salon was next. I didn't ever go in there, definitely a girly place. In the old world, I'd been dragged along a few times when my mom went, so I knew what everything was. The smell of nail polish remover made me cover my nose. In front of a mirrored counter sat a hair-cutting stall with a nearby hair dryer. I looked in the mirror and saw a face.

I jumped, and then felt stupid when I saw what it was. A nearby shelf held a row of practice heads, plastic heads with real hair. I exhaled, surprised at myself for being so on edge.

There were also two pedicure chairs with attached foot-baths. A manicure table sat nearby, and glass shelves filled with bottles of nail polish ran along one whole wall. I shook my head and backed out the door.

The laundry and sewing room was next. The room had a bleachy smell. Stacked washer-dryer units were lined up next to one another, next to large sinks. One of the dryers was running, and something metallic clicked every time the clothes flipped. Across from them was a long table that held several types of sewing machines. Thick bolts of fabric were piled on shelves behind the table. Boring. I shut the door and moved on.

Through the glass door of the dance studio, I saw Lexie practicing ballet. Her hair was twisted in a dancer's top-knot, and she wore a black leotard and pink toe shoes. (Her wardrobe was slightly more extensive than mine.) In the old world, she attended a performing arts school, where she studied both ballet and piano. Since Eddy and I went to a Chinese immersion school on the other side of the city, our schedules were different enough that I really only saw Lexie during summer vacation. Before the Compound, anyway.

I stood there, watching for a while. She danced with a confidence she never showed other times. Lexie tended to cover up her insecurities with her lousy attitude. My reasoning was her being insecure came from being adopted. From how she treated us, though, you'd think she didn't give a crap about any of us. Except Dad. He could do no wrong where she was concerned.

And he ate it up, all her attention. Like he didn't already have people groveling at his feet every day. Lexie would never go against Dad. It was a little ridiculous really, how she went along with everything he said. Mom had no sway with her. I hated that Lexie could get Dad to go against Mom's wishes just to please her, his oldest daughter.

Still, I did like to watch Lexie dance. Even at her school recitals Eddy and I would quit fidgeting when she was onstage. As I watched her through the door, there was something about the long lines of her lithe body, the strength of her jumps, and the grace of her movements. She seemed so focused, so lost in the dance, like nothing else existed.

I wished there were something like that for me, something more than free throws and tai chi that I could get lost in.

Lexie stopped when she noticed me and stood with one hand on her jutted-out hip, the other holding up a middle finger.

Acknowledging her greeting with a wave, I called out in Mandarin, *"Si san ba."* Years ago I'd told her it was an affectionate term for a "big sister." I'd have to find a new phrase if she ever discovered what nasty word it actually meant.

On my way once more, I passed the rock-climbing wall and media room. Next door was the music studio. Mom was playing cello, so I slipped in, sinking to the floor to listen. Mozart.

Her back was to me, and her long hair hung straight down in an even plait. My mother was the gentlest person

I'd ever met. Gentle in her manner, her voice, her touch. I imagined that Clea Sheridan Yanakakis had never mustered up even an iota of bad feeling toward anyone. However, her gentle nature didn't mean she wasn't intense. One only had to watch her play cello for a short while to understand her depth. You don't have to be loud or forceful to take up a lot of space in the world.

Her mother wasn't as quiet or as gentle. Gram was part Hawaiian and half Chinese, along with an eighth each of overbearing and opinionated. We loved her, of course, even though her demeanor wasn't anything like Mom's. Gram was that way for a reason. As she told it, at one time she was as quiet as Mom. She married a music professor, had Mom, and was quite content. Their blissful life changed when Mom was five and her dad was killed in a car accident.

From what I knew, he left them with insufficient funds, and Gram was lonely. In addition, she thought Mom should have a male influence. Gram remarried, a man whose name I never knew.

The whole story never came my way, just bits through closed doors when I was supposed to be asleep, merged with things Eddy and Lexie heard. Putting them together, we determined the guy was a loser, demanding and scheming toward Gram, verbally abusive toward Mom. Gram finally kicked him out, even though it left her strapped for money once again. Mom came out of it quiet and sensitive, but she was not without resources. She had inherited her father's talent for music.

I loved to listen to her, especially moments like this, when she didn't know she had an audience. Somehow she seemed freer, more at ease. A way she never seemed around my dad.

She set her bow aside for a moment to switch sheet music.

I ducked down in case she turned around.

She started again. Debussy. The music gave me goose bumps.

Even if she had been completely void of talent, she still would have taken away people's breath with her looks. I saw it in their eyes, whenever she came to one of my school events. Oh, at first the teachers and the other parents were always disappointed when my dad didn't show up, but I think Mom ended up being more interesting to them.

Her father's Irish and Scottish background had combined with Gram's ancestry, leaving Mom with dark hair, deep green eyes, and slightly Polynesian features. She'd walk in the room in her expensive clothes. Classic, elegant, never flashy, but still she'd stand out. I was proud that I had the prettiest mom.

Funny, we had all inherited Mom's looks. Except Eddy and I had brown eyes like Gram. Even though Lexie was adopted, she had the same dark hair as Mom. None of us looked like my dad with his fair features. At least the four of us didn't.

As for the ones in the yellow room, I couldn't say. I'd never seen them.

Trying not to make any noise as I stood up, I left without revealing my presence. In the carpeted section of the Compound, there was only one room left: the chapel.

For as long as I could remember, Dad had been adamant about our churchgoing. During my childhood, unless we were dying or close to it, our butts were in a Methodist pew every Sunday. I knew more Bible verses than any kid had a right to. And I'm sure the church loved getting my father's tithes. The minister certainly seemed pleased to see us arrive every Sunday.

Even in the Compound we remembered the Sabbath day and kept it holy. For the first several years, each Sunday, as well as every Christmas Eve, Dad delivered a brief sermon. We sang a few hymns as Lexie accompanied us on the organ, then Mom read some Bible verses. Those terse moments of religion were sufficient enough to feel that God was with us in the Compound. We never had any reason to doubt that He was. And then, with no explanation, Dad quit holding chapel services just like he quit working out. So I hadn't been in there for a while.

The chapel had four rows of carved wooden pews facing a small altar with a wooden pulpit. A large gold cross hung on the wall behind the pulpit, and an organ sat off to one side. Heavy purple curtains framed the setting, and except for the small size, it looked much like the church we attended in Seattle.

It felt strange being in there alone. The room was so hushed and empty.

I stepped onto the pulpit. I'd never been up there before. Dad's Bible was on top and I opened it. A sheet of blue lined paper fell out. In Dad's handwriting was a list of several items regarding banking and stocks. The title was composed of two words:

TELL PHIL

Tell Phil? Why would Dad have a note to his accountant sitting in his Bible? The date was a few months ago, but the year must have been wrong. It was old, of course. Had to be. Guess he needed to be reminded of the old world as much as we did. Or maybe he'd done it on purpose, written a note to his accountant like he did in the old world a dozen times a day. Maybe he needed to pretend in order to feel a little normal once in a while, just like I did.

I put the note back where I found it.

A cursory search of the rest of the room revealed nothing. Not that I knew what I was looking for. I left.

At the end of the carpeted section of the Compound stood a double door. As I stepped through, a rush of air hit me. The ceiling was twenty-five feet over my head. The entire space went as far as I could see to my sides and front, and was open except for various walls and doors every now and then—a warehouse. There were storage areas, shelves that stretched all the way to the ceiling, and the freezers, twenty of them.

I hopped into the golf cart sitting near the door and drove, stopping randomly at one of the storage rooms. I opened the door. Of course I'd been in all of them before many times, to get toilet paper or laundry detergent. Had I ever really considered how Dad had done it all?

The Compound itself must have taken years to build, not even counting all the planning. How do you know how much toilet paper you'll use in fifteen years? Also, how could a project like this, headed up by my dad, not make it on CNN? If I had worked on the Compound, then found out we were under attack, this is the first place I would have headed.

The answer was probably money, which my dad had loads of. Power, too. He probably made everyone sign a confidentiality agreement and paid them a lot to do so. It was sort of a constant in the old world. My father had the means to get whatever he wanted.

That was just how things were. And we all knew it.

I glanced at my watch and realized I was late for chores, so I headed to the very back of the Compound.

My main job was to run the hydroponic garden, an enormous open room where vegetables grew in troughs of water, relying on artificial sunlight to grow more rapidly than in traditional soil gardens. I'd learned about hydroponics at a local co-op we went to every Saturday on the outside. While I learned how to grow vegetables, Eddy learned about livestock and poultry. My mom learned how to bake bread, can vegetables. Part of Dad's planning, I'd come to realize, that we all have a role in the subsistence world of the Compound.

The tomatoes, lettuce, and red bell peppers were close to another harvest. I started some more seedlings by pushing seeds into small squares of sponges. One row of grow light bulbs flickered.

I held my breath.

They came back on. Stayed on.

I breathed again, relieved.

After nine months in the Compound, some bulbs had gone out. I replaced them, but the light didn't look the same. After checking the storage room with the supply of grow light bulbs, I found a nasty surprise. More than three-fourths of them were normal fluorescent bulbs, no good for growing anything.

Depending on how long the grow bulbs lasted, our supply of vegetables would run out around the time I turned eighteen, if not sooner. So I had good reason to panic every time those bulbs flickered. Especially when I took into account the rest of the food situation. And that was something I tried not to think about.

CHAPTER FIVE

I FINISHED MY WORK IN THE HYDROPONICS AND HEADED TO the computer room to do some schoolwork. We had the best computers, of course, at least they were the best available when we entered the Compound. Dad had started his company on his own, building computers, and he still created prototypes for new ones, each better than the last. I could only imagine how many millions of dollars the latest model would have made. It was weird sometimes to think about money when there was no need for it in the Compound. I guess I'd always been tuned into it, though, knowing we'd had so much.

Our computers were loaded with educational software, all programmed to work at the user's pace with an infinite level of endless subjects. Although I had just turned fifteen, I was on my first year of college studies. This wonder boy was gifted in math and sciences, big shocker there. Plus I still studied Mandarin.

Lexie was on her first year of college, studying literature and Greek. I'm pretty sure she would have been more of a vapid socialite in the old world. In the Compound she studied, but only the subjects she liked. She refused to do any math or sciences and Dad let her get away with it. Perhaps he thought it was a waste of time nurturing the other areas. Most likely Lexie just got her way with him, once again.

I spread my books out on the table, wondering what it would actually be like to have to study in a room full of people, to only have a small allotted space. Not the entire room, as I did. I never had to tell anyone to pipe down so I could concentrate, that's for sure.

A word problem in calculus was totally confusing me, so I finally gave in and decided to ask Dad for some help. His office was set apart from the rest of the rooms down a private alcove, and always locked up tight whenever he wasn't there. I'd never been inside.

I reached his office and knocked on the door. It clicked open. He must not have shut it tight. He'd likely just stepped out for a moment, knowing none of us were usually around his office that time of day.

"Dad?"

No answer.

I pushed the door a bit with my foot. I took another glance down the hallway to make sure it was empty, and then stepped onto the threshold. The smell of pipe tobacco hit my nose as my quick gaze absorbed the décor.

A rush of déjà vu flooded me as I realized the office was

identical to Dad's office in our house in Seattle. A thicker coating of dust on the stack of old *National Geographic*s was the only thing that was different. A huge chair on wheels still sat behind the richly polished paneled desk. Three separate flat-monitor computers, a wall of clocks with several time zones, and his favorite Seattle Seahawks football phone. Everything almost nearly the same. Except for the padlocked door on the far side of the room.

"Eli?"

I'm sure I looked guilty when I twisted toward him, but I tried to be casual. "Dad, hey, I need to ask you something."

"What the hell are you doing in here?" His frown was fierce.

My words stammered out. "I—I wasn't doing anything."

He looked beyond me, into the office, like he was making sure everything was still there. "You're not allowed in here."

I took a breath, and then stated in an even tone, "I wasn't in your office, Dad. I just need your help." I held up a notebook, revealing scribbled equations.

"Oh." He waited for me to pass by him, into the hallway. Better than anyone else, Dad understood the need for me to not be touched. Not that he'd ever really been the touchy-feely type, anyway. He shut the office door behind him, tight this time. "Let's take a look."

Back in the computer lab I explained how I'd tried to solve the problem, unsuccessfully.

Dad rubbed his chin and squinted at my writing. "Did you convert it to math?"

I held out my notes. "That's what I'm trying to do. The quantities aren't fixed."

"Did you name them by a variable?"

I shook my head. "Didn't get that far."

"Let's try a similar one." He jotted down a complicated equation. His mind seemed to work so fast that his fingers couldn't keep up.

I tried to solve for x, but couldn't figure it out. Dad being so close made me nervous, not able to think straight.

"Come on, Eli. Think." He solved it as I watched. "You can do this."

The answer dawned on me and I smacked my forehead with one hand. "Stupid. That was one of my first ideas but it didn't seem right."

Dad shrugged. "You should have gone with your first instinct. It's usually right." He stood. "I need to get back to work."

☢

AFTER DAD LEFT, I HAD TROUBLE CONCENTRATING ON THE rest of my studies. Why was Dad so freaked about me being in his office? Before we came here, if he was working on new software or a new computer design, he was doubly cautious about security. But why would he be paranoid down here? Who was I going to tell? And what was behind that locked door? Other than the room behind the yellow door, I'd toured the entire Compound so many times I knew every room. Or so I thought.

At first I'd assumed our close proximity over the past six years would have made me closer to Dad. He no longer had the huge demands of his company. In the old world, our time with him had been scheduled, as if it were an appointment written down in some shiny black book. We had dinner as a family at six every night, spent an hour or so in the library or den, maybe played a game or something, then at nine he bid us adieu and headed off to his study.

Nothing had really changed that much. He still did exactly what he wanted and none of us questioned him. Maybe the hardest fact to swallow was that, despite his being my father, I didn't know any more about the man than the general public might find out by reading his biography.

Rex Yanakakis, adopted as a baby, then orphaned when he was nineteen, used his genius mind and inheritance to get a degree in computer science at MIT, and then start his own company. Not wanting to forget his roots, he supported the orphanage he'd been sent to as a baby. They ended up naming it for him. Quite a slick move, I'd say. It basically guaranteed his continued generous support.

At age twenty-seven, when his company was already on its way to the top, he saw my mom play in the Seattle Symphony and didn't stop sending her white roses by the dozen until she agreed to see him. I can imagine the situation was attractive to her. To be raised with hardly any money, then grow up to be courted by one of the richest, most powerful men in the world? I'm sure the thought of a life with that kind of security had to hold a huge appeal.

They got married, built a thirty-room estate overlooking Puget Sound, immediately adopted one-year-old Lexie from the Yanakakis Home for Children, and then had three kids the regular way. They lived the sweet life. Happily ever after and all that crap.

That's the Rex Yanakakis the world knew.

What Rex Yanakakis did I know?

My dad was never one of those dads you could ask for a quarter if you saw a gumball machine. Instead he had one of those black American Express cards not available to the general public. Gumball machines didn't have slots for those.

My dad was never one of those dads who raked piles of leaves to jump in with their kids. He worked long hours most of the year, so his idea of quality time was a two-week trip twice a year, usually to somewhere exotic like Tahiti or Morocco. And there was usually another reason for going, like the time he "acquired" the software company in Rabat, or bought an uninhabited, uncharted island in the South Pacific. Our "vacations" always included some kind of business transaction.

Except for that last trip, a camping trip, the one that ended with us coming here, to the Compound. We just happened to be on Dad's three thousand acres in eastern Washington when our nation was attacked.

Even though Dad always told us the Compound could be reached by helicopter from our estate in under that ubiquitous forty minutes, I thought that was cutting it a bit close. I remember thinking how lucky we were to be at the cabin with our RV, so close to the Compound we had heard so much about right as the nightmare began.

But we were not lucky that we were away from the cabin, a ways away, when we discovered Terese had smuggled a stray kitten into the RV.

We were not lucky when Eddy's allergies flared up.

Not lucky that his medicine was back at the cabin.

Not lucky that Gram had to drive back to the cabin in the Range Rover to get the medicine while the rest of us went to bed.

Not lucky Eddy climbed in the back of the SUV without anyone knowing.

And definitely not lucky that some country decided that moment was the right one to launch a nuclear attack, sending us careening across the flat landscape in the RV.

The rest of it comes to me in a series of black-and-white flashes:

Dad slamming on the brakes. Grabbing Terese.

Dad shouting at the rest of us. Get out! Run! Run! Run!

Following behind him in the dark. Stumbling over rocks in the middle of nowhere. Mom running, too, helping us up.

The night. So dark. Chilly. My family simply manic shadows alongside me.

Stopping at a hole in the ground. Not a hole. A hatch.

Dad pushing us, making us climb down. Dad staying up on top.

Me screaming for Cocoa. Dad promising to find her.

Me going with the others. Down into a room. Stairs. So many stairs.

Descending. Descending. Descending.

To the silver door. A gaping mouth wanting to swallow us.

Waiting. Waiting. Precious minutes ticking.

Too much time.

Mom leading us through the silver door.

Dad returning.

Me screaming.

Silver door closing. Loud. Reverberating in my head.

Gram gone.

Eddy gone.

World? Gone.

That wasn't all of it. My mind censored out the worst part. The part where I was selfish. The part where I would do anything to get what I wanted. Even if it meant leaving my brother out of our only hope for survival. Our sanctuary.

My dad was the type of dad who spent a billion dollars on that sanctuary so his family could survive a nuclear attack. That should have been enough for most people.

Problem was I had never been most kind of people.

I would have rather had a dad with change jingling in his pocket; one who would have spent the last forty minutes of the world raking leaves for his kids to jump in, so that they perished in one loud, bright instant, giggles still bubbling up from their bellies, never suspecting a thing.

Yeah, well. Tough luck, rich boy.

CHAPTER SIX

My dreams that night, like so many other nights, were of food. Cheeseburgers, loaded with bacon and mayo and ketchup. Seasoned curly fries, greasy and dripping in mustard. Milk shakes, thick slices of strawberry cheesecake, hot fudge sundaes.

When I woke up, my pillow was wet with drool and my stomach growled. I hated waking up like that, immediately reminded of our pathetic food situation.

It hadn't always been bad. In the beginning we had plenty to eat. An enormous open room near the hydroponics housed the poultry and livestock. Without Eddy to do the job, caring for them fell to me. We had five Holsteins, all with suckling calves. With their soft fur, slippery noses, and sandpaper tongues, the calves were so loveable that it helped me not miss Cocoa so much.

Their pen was a smaller version of a corral you'd see on a ranch. Smelled like one as well. Every day, wishing I could worm my way out of it, I grudgingly held my breath as I scooped up their manure and hauled it to one of the incinerators. I gave the animals water, and then carried grain by bucketfuls to their trough. The trough sat near a water tank that I filled with a hose from a nearby spigot.

The chickens were not as fun as the cows. I sprinkled their corn, brought clean water, and rushed out of the henhouse. I hated the putrid stench of chicken crap. Most days I gathered eggs. Those were a treat, especially when Mom made them into cheese omelets.

One entire room of the warehouse was devoted to feed for the animals. Should it dwindle, Dad explained, we would butcher the cows and make do without milk and the cheese and butter that Mom made. Even though it would mean less shoveling for me, I chose not to think about that day, counting on the feed to last.

Between the dairy and poultry products, produce from the garden, and freezers full of meat, we ate well.

For the first seven months.

The morning it all changed started out like any other. Life had become routine, almost like we'd always lived in the Compound.

With an orange wheelbarrow, I hauled a new bag of feed out of the storeroom and poured it into the cows' trough. They dug in with gusto as usual, the calves nursing as their mothers chewed, their crunching loud. The chickens were ecstatic when I fed them, their ruffling feathers and cackling driving me nuts.

The next day I went to feed them. I was puzzled. Neither

the chickens nor cows touched the food I gave them. The cows dripped saliva while the calves suckled.

I went to get Dad.

He wasn't that up on hanging out with the livestock. His nose wrinkled the minute he walked in the room, and his eyes were glued to the ground as he took ginger steps around any dirt I might have missed when I cleaned up, even though he wore knee-high muck boots.

Dad wasn't sure what to make of the cows' behavior. "They probably have to adjust to this place, too. They'll be back to normal in a day or so."

Later, I went back to check. The cows stood there, panting and drooling. The calves lay on their sides, still.

I rested my hand on one.

The fur was still soft. But the body was stiff and cold. The calves were dead. All of them.

And it was quiet in there. Too quiet.

I realized what was missing. Cackling. Inside the hen-house, I found all the chickens, unmoving and lifeless.

I ran to get Dad, and then struggled to keep up as we raced back. By then a cow was on her side. "What the hell is wrong with you?" he hissed.

My mouth opened to defend myself, to tell him I'd done everything the way I was supposed to. I was afraid to speak.

Dad held a hand to the cow's heaving flank. I realized his words were directed at her, not me.

He grabbed a couple of stainless steel buckets from the stack. He put some water in one and a few handfuls of grain in the other and took them to his lab. I followed to watch him.

He readied the microscope and his other equipment, then set to work. Inspected first, the water ended up being fine; it was the same we all drank.

I went to check on the cows and decided to stay with them. One by one they dropped to their forelegs, then fell onto their sides. I was with them through the afternoon. One by one, they died.

Back in the lab, I found Dad deep in concentration. He didn't seem to notice me as he studied the information that compiled on his computer screen. At last his analysis was complete. "No, no, no. No, No, NO." Dad leaned on the counter, holding his head in his hands. "Traces of rat poison." His exact next words escape me. I do know he shouted something about the cows and swore. A lot.

I took all the dead chickens to the incinerator with the orange wheelbarrow, which I christened The Hearse. Dad sliced up the large animals with equipment from the meat processing room. The grinding whine stayed in my head for days.

☢

I COULDN'T GO BACK TO SLEEP. MY ALARM HADN'T GONE OFF yet, so I stayed in bed and daydreamed, as I often did, about things I used to take for granted. The smell of Cocoa after her bath, and the way she tore around the house, rolling on every carpet in sight, grunting. I felt her then, her body on top of my feet, her warmth seeping through the covers. She was my phantom limb.

For six years I'd tried not to dwell on thoughts of her or anyone else too long. It was better to separate the old world from the new. It was better to stay cold and detached.

Actually, I was getting good at cold and detached. Too good.

I shivered, and pulled the covers up tight.

I often wondered about the cows and how it all could have happened. Could one of the workers have sabotaged the food supply? And the grow bulbs in hydroponics. Could someone have put fluorescent ones in their place on purpose? A disgruntled worker who knew the job was coming to an end? An envious working stiff who hated the thought of his own family dying while the Yanakakis clan lived out nuclear winter in luxury?

I hid my face in my hands, rubbing away at the sleepiness.

Dad had planned well, of course. But even he had made mistakes. I crunched my last tortilla chip when I was eleven. Swallowed my last Mountain Dew when I was thirteen. Peanut butter ran out when I was fourteen, the jelly soon after. We each learned to hoard. Underneath my bed, a dozen Snickers called to me. True, the one I ate on my birthday was white around the edges and tasted rather off. Still, I saved the rest. I liked knowing they were there.

Dad had stockpiled tons, literally, of food. But even he couldn't extend the shelf life. Most canned goods were fresh for three, four years tops; wheat and honey were the only two foods with an indefinite shelf life. Trust me on that.

The meat in the freezers became increasingly inedible

in Year Three. We'd been vegetarian since I was thirteen. Not by choice. I'd have given a few body parts for a burger and fries.

Sometimes when I thought about this place called Uncle Barney's we used to go to, I'd get a little choked up. They made these incredible Monte Cristo sandwiches with layers of smoked turkey and honey ham and cheddar and Swiss, drenched in beer batter, then deep fried. Nice, eh? Rich kid pines away for food, and doesn't shed a tear for the brother he killed.

My stomach growled then, at just the thought of meat. I resisted the temptation to reach under the bed for a Snickers. Instead I got up to do my tai chi. I began the motions. I tried. I couldn't stop thinking about the food.

How food used to be fun.

Not anymore.

Meals had become scientific, every bite like a mathematical equation, each integer blending together to create an adequate sum, product, solution. This bite and that equaled proper nutrition.

My gaze fell to the oak dresser and the industrial-size bottle of vitamins I took by the handful. No substitute for real food, they were close to expiring. We wouldn't starve as long as the honey and wheat lasted. Malnutrition *could* become an issue, inviting related ailments such as scurvy and rickets. Nice.

My right calf muscle felt tight. I stopped to stretch. My hands kneaded the sinewy lower half of my leg.

Of course there was a safety net: MREs, meals ready to

eat. Dad laid in a huge stock, thousands purchased from a military supply place. Way to go, Pops.

My concentration was shot, so I gave up on tai chi and went to take a preworkout shower. Thanks to Dad's high-tech water heaters, at least we had plenty of that. I stepped in, hoping the water would wash away my thoughts. Didn't work.

I didn't get it, how he could go through the entire planning process of the Compound, and then screw up the most important thing. I respected him for the effort, of course, who else could have pulled this off, but still. To screw up something as basic as the food supply?

The blasted saga of the MREs wouldn't leave me alone.

Stored at 60 degrees, they have a shelf life of 130 months, give or take a few. They would last for at least ten years. Stored at 60 degrees. The thermostat in the MRE storage room malfunctioned. Rising to 90 degrees, it stayed there for over six weeks before anyone noticed. Stored at 90 degrees, MREs have a shelf life of 55 months.

We began eating up the MREs while they were still good. Good being a relative term. I suspected they were always crappy, even in their prime. Not much variation there. Macaroni hot dish. Beef stew. Chop suey. There was, however, variation in how they were prepared, as stated by the official instructions. I'd read them so many times while I ate that they were ingrained in my mind:

Place unopened pouch in warm water for 5–10 minutes.
Unopened pouch may be laid on a warm surface.

Lay unopened pouch in direct sunlight. Not much chance of that down here.

Place unopened pouch inside your shirt, allow your body temperature to warm your MRE.

I was surprised they left out: *Place unopened pouch on ground and pee on it.*

As the water ran hot down my body, I had another thought. Could the thermostat in the MRE room have been sabotaged as well? Who would wish us such ill will? Stupid question. Billions of people. For no other reason than for all that we possessed. Especially our survival.

I switched off the water and stepped out, grabbing a towel.

If someone had tampered with our food, they never could have imagined the depths we would sink to in order to remedy the situation. Because soon after the MRE disaster, Dad made a decision necessary for his family's survival; a decision a normal person could never have lived with.

A decision I had to live with every day.

A decision I had to think about, whether I wanted to or not, every time I walked by that yellow door.

CHAPTER SEVEN

I TOOK A SIP OF WATER BEFORE SHOVING THE BOTTLE IN THE holder on the treadmill. Then I stuck my headphones in my ears and increased the volume on my MP3 player. The White Stripes blasted in my ears as I set the treadmill's hilly course for six miles. Running on the treadmill probably wasn't as fun as running outside. I didn't know any different. And it was the time I set aside for just listening to music.

Despite being a devoted fan of Bob Dylan and similar musicians, Dad had stocked the CD collection with every genre, including music more off the mainstream. Grunge bands, punk, alternative, indie rock.

He'd actually been selecting it for me, since the media library was so big and I didn't know what to look for half the time. When he managed to find some bands I liked, I had to transfer them to my player. No problem. I was made of time.

My mom came into the gym as I hit mile three. She raised her eyebrows. "If I can hear your music, it's too loud."

The music was too loud to hear her, but she'd said that so many times I could read her lips. The volume went down.

Naturally her balance was a bit awkward. She clambered onto the recumbent bike. Her long hair was in a ponytail and she wore an oversize YK T-shirt and black velour bottoms, the waist folded in order to accommodate her huge, pregnant belly.

She started pedaling, and then smiled at me. "I'm feeling cumbersome."

I didn't answer. My mom and I never really talked. To clarify, she talked to me all the time. I usually just grunted and nodded my head.

The only sounds besides the music were the whine of the treadmill and the whir of the bike.

"Today I'm craving peanut butter and banana sandwiches. On white bread even, if you can believe that."

I didn't feel like talking about her cravings. I had plenty of my own.

Mom pushed some stray hair out of her eyes. "Eli, you should visit them one day."

I lost my footing and had to grab on to the rail to keep from falling off the treadmill. Did she say that just to get me to talk? It worked, because once I had found my rhythm again, I responded. "How can you say that? You know what they are."

Mom fiddled with the control buttons. They beeped along with her words. "I know what your father thinks they are."

She'd never broached the subject of the Supplements with me before, even though it was always there, hanging over our heads. She probably thought it wasn't worth it, me being the cold loner that I was. Why would I give a crap about them? But maybe her catching me in Eddy's room changed things. She'd figured out, despite my trying not to show it, that I did have feelings.

What the hell, the cards were on the table. It was the time to ask what I'd always wondered, but never had the guts to talk about. "Why did you do it? Agree to it?"

Mom stretched her arms, then folded them behind her head and leaned back, still pedaling. "It didn't start out to be . . . Your father said we might be the only ones left. Or some of the few left. And we owed it to the world to give it the biggest population we could."

I rolled my eyes. "And you bought that story?"

Her eyes narrowed. "He wouldn't do it unless I agreed entirely. And I understood." She set a hand on her bump. "Obviously I was the key."

That much was clear. "But why? I mean, the situation changed once the food supply . . . was compromised. It was no longer about rebuilding the planet, was it? You knew what he wanted to do."

Her shoulders went up and down once. "I love you and your sisters so much. Your father knew that; I'd do anything for you. After losing Eddy, your gram . . . I was just in a daze. It seemed like I was doing the right thing, saving the children I had left, securing your future. Something Eddy didn't have anymore. Now, seeing them every day—"

"Supplements, Mom. That's what they are. That's all they are." I picked the bottle out of the holder and took a cold drink.

She sighed, and her tone softened. "No, Eli. That's not all they are."

I turned up my music. With one motion, I undid my ponytail and let my hair drift over my face. I had nothing more to say to her.

Mom finished and took her time standing. She leaned toward me, her hands reaching on either side of my head.

I tried to move away as she grabbed the headphones out of my ears. "There's a lot you don't know, Eli." She backed off, her eyes looking down.

I wanted to spit the words out. "Like what?"

She tried to find my eyes behind the curtain of hair. "I'm not sure, because there are things I don't know, either." She took a brief glimpse around before lowering her voice. "Your father has always kept things from me, even before we came in here. Lately I feel it even more. He's got secrets, Eli."

Her voice changed, lost its gentle tone. "And if those secrets affect you or your sisters or . . . the others?" With one sweep of her hand, she wiped the sweat off her forehead. "He may be my husband, but I don't trust him. Not anymore."

"Why not?" I'd never had this kind of conversation with my mom. It felt strange, having her open up so much. But I wanted to know.

"The other day I was in the bedroom. My feet smell bad when I'm pregnant, did I ever tell you that?"

I shook my head. Of course she'd never told me that. We hadn't had a talk this long for the last six years. I slowed the treadmill down so I was walking.

"Only when I'm pregnant. It's odd. So I got a bottle of talcum powder to sprinkle in my tennies, before I came to work out. But I'm so clumsy now, and I tripped on the carpet and dropped the bottle. The powder went all over the rug, everywhere. I pulled out the hose from the central vacuum to clean it up, but my hands were slippery, because I'd just put on some lotion. The hose snapped out of my hands and hit the headboard, knocking down the painting."

"The Monet."

She smiled at me. "You remember."

I nodded.

"I always knew it was merely a reproduction. How could it be anything else? We were camping, right? So far from home. There was no time to bring the original. But when I lifted the painting to hang it back up, I looked at it closely for the first time."

Her smiled faded. "Do you remember the Monet?"

I nodded. The painting was of a woman wearing a white dress, viewed from behind, and her shoulders were bare, her hair piled on top of her head. The woman could have been my mother.

"Your father gave it to me the day you and Eddy were born. Could you imagine how it felt? To come from where I did, and then be given a painting worth millions, such a beautiful piece, to have for my very own? I looked at it every day for nearly nine years." Mom's eyes misted a bit with the memory.

"Once we came here, I never so much as glanced at the one on my bedroom wall. I didn't want to see a reproduction, because everything in the Compound was that; the air and the light and even our daily life. They were all just reproductions of the real thing. But when I picked the Monet up to hang it on the wall, I did look at it. For the first time, I really looked."

She paused, resting one hand on her belly as the other still held my headphones.

"The Monet is real. The Monet hanging on the wall of my bedroom in this godforsaken Compound, three stories underground, is the real thing. How do you explain that, Eli? How do you explain that?" Her eyebrows went up.

My mouth dropped. Was she waiting for me to give her an answer? Because I only had questions. "What? How can that be?"

"If your father had time to switch the paintings, it would mean he knew, somehow, he'd been warned of the attack. And if that's true, why wouldn't he have told everyone? Why wouldn't we have come here earlier with your brother and my mother?"

"Did you ask Dad?"

She shook her head. "I have to wait for the right time.

And I don't think that's now." Her hand reached out with my headphones. "And he's wrong, dead wrong, if he thinks I will let him go through with any plan involving . . . involving anything so horrendous."

She handed me the headphones. I watched her leave. The treadmill beeped as the incline moved upward, starting a long ascent. I realized it was a mistake to assume gentleness was akin with weakness.

I turned off the treadmill, hair hanging in my eyes, sweat running down my neck as I stood there panting, thinking. Mom's mistrust of my dad, Terese's rant in the gym, how could I be such a fool? For six years I'd been feeling sorry for myself and shutting out my family as much as I could, going through the motions, convincing myself we were the lucky ones.

Everyone on earth perished, right? Didn't they? With all of Dad's technology, wouldn't he want to know what was happening aboveground?

He was keeping something from us.

Something big.

I skipped lifting weights and my shower, too. I had to get back to Dad's office. I would make up a story about a chemistry experiment gone awry. I stopped in my room to grab a notebook. My laptop was in the chem lab and I didn't feel like running all the way there and back, so I picked up the laptop I'd found in Eddy's room and took that, too.

Dad's office door was shut. Through the thick wood, I could just barely hear him talking to himself. His tone sounded perturbed.

Suddenly my plan didn't seem so great after all. I didn't want to disturb him in the middle of work, especially if he was frustrated. The moment had to be right, and I sat down on the floor to the side of the door to wait. I tied back my hair, then pulled out the laptop from Eddy's room.

The laptop came on. Out of habit, I clicked on the Internet icon. Because it was there. I waited for the message to come up and tell me I was not connected to the world.

But it didn't.

Instead, another message came.

Wireless Network Now Connected.

My jaw dropped. "What the hell?" Words formed in my mouth. I fought the urge to call out to Dad. But I remembered the promise I made to Mom, the promise to keep the laptop a secret.

The leather of his chair squeaked. "Is someone out there?"

I shut the laptop and cleared my throat. "Yeah, Dad, me. I wondered if you could help me with some experiments." I stood up, scrambling to cover the laptop with my notebook. "Later's fine, though, if you're too busy."

The door swung open. "Now's fine." Dad stood there in his usual jeans and T-shirt, a sheaf of papers under his arm.

I held my breath, trying to resist the urge to look down at Eddy's laptop, hoping that, half covered by the papers, it resembled my other laptop enough to not draw his attention.

Dad moved toward me as the door shut, but I still got a glimpse of his office.

Although it was infinitesimal, I noticed something. My father had always been meticulous. He believed in a place for everything, everything in its place. No variations; things were always in their spot as if glued there. So when my glance revealed something out of place, it didn't take long to notice what item was not where it was supposed to be: the Seattle Seahawks football phone.

We headed toward the lab, Dad poring over a sheet of paper as he walked. He went into the hallway restroom, and I took the opportunity to open the laptop back up, see if the message was still there. There *was* a message. Just not the one I wanted to see.

Wireless Server Not Available.

I shut the laptop. Had it been my imagination? Did I want to see something so badly that I hallucinated? In the lab, I slipped the laptop in a drawer before Dad could notice it.

"Oh, Eli. Here." Dad handed me a CD.

Still freaked by the laptop, I just thanked him for the CD. I didn't look at it until I was back in my room. The band was Cake. Never heard of them. The song started and my pencil started tapping.

> *Reluctantly crouched at the starting line*
> *Engines pumping and thumping in time*
> *The green light flashes, the flags go up*
> *Churning and burning they yearn for the cup*

I liked it. Which wasn't always the case with the songs Dad gave me.

The song ended and I ejected to find out the name of it.

The door stuck, trapping the CD halfway out. I noticed the label on top of the CD had an edge sticking up. Took me a little while to get a good enough grip before I could yank it out.

The label was simply a printout, made with high-quality photo paper, somehow heat sealed or laminated. Tearing it all the way off revealed a recordable CD. In black Sharpie, the name of the band was written in Dad's handwriting.

CAKE

A date followed: a very recent date. My hand slapped over my mouth.

How was that possible? How in the hell did I come to be holding a copy of a CD made only weeks ago?

It was like the dated note I'd found in the chapel. But I wasn't going to dismiss this one so easily.

I'd been holding my breath. It came out in a rush.

Unless we always had the music and Dad simply made a copy of it, adding the date as he always did.

I dug through the stack of CDs on my desk, all given to me by my father. For the next hour, I used the sharp side of some scissors to scrape away at several labels. All fake. All PC-recorded CDs with handwritten names and dates.

All the dates well after we were in the Compound.

In the media room, I found the catalog that listed every CD we had with us. I took it back to my room.

My finger tracked down the list as I perused it for any of the groups on my desk. I went through the entire stack, dozens. There wasn't a listing for any of them. This was no small omission on my dad's part. This was colossal.

CHAPTER EIGHT

I WAS AWAKE ALL NIGHT, THINKING. I WAS PISSED, PISSED AT the possibility that my father was keeping things from me, maybe even lying. And if that was true, I would be even more upset at myself for being such a dupe, just taking things lying down, believing everything he said.

But I was also afraid of what would happen when I did ask him for the truth. What if he didn't give it to me? Worse, what if he did and it wasn't what I wanted to hear?

But I knew what Eddy would do. I also knew he wasn't here to do it for me.

Right away the next morning, before I could chicken out, I pounded on Dad's office door.

He opened it. "I'm busy, Eli. Can it wait?" There were deep circles under his eyes and his jaw was covered with stubble. Must have been one of his sleepless nights. He was wrapped in a plaid fleece blanket in his chair, leaning out the door just enough to see me.

I handed him the Cake CD and waited.

"What's wrong? Doesn't it play?" He noticed the missing label, the date written in his own handwriting. His face paled.

"Dad, I think . . ." I suddenly wasn't sure what I thought. My carefully considered argument abandoned me. So, heart pounding, I stammered out what I could. "I've felt for a while like something isn't right." A bit of a lie, since it had taken Terese to open my eyes.

Dad opened the door wider and scooted his chair back to his desk. He set the CD down, then leaned back in his chair. I couldn't believe he was being so open, ushering me into his inner sanctum. I froze, and wondered if I looked as dumbstruck as I felt. He motioned for me to sit down on the couch, where a pillow and blanket lay, and I realized he'd been sleeping there. I moved them aside to make room.

I sat, then untucked my hair from behind my ears and let it fall forward over my eyes. My eyes strayed to the padlocked door, but I dismissed it for the moment. One thing at a time.

Dad removed his reading glasses. He took his time folding them before he placed them on his desk. He yawned and pulled the blanket up around him.

Inside, I screamed at him to get on with it.

"Eli, there's something you don't know."

You think? I remained silent.

"I've always told you the Compound is wired for communication. Of course, I never expected to use it, given that all communication would be decimated: phones, Internet, fax. But a while ago, I got a wireless Internet signal."

My mouth gaped.

Dad smiled, nodding. "I know, I know, it felt like a miracle. I didn't want to say anything."

Even though I knew he'd been keeping stuff from us, that revelation threw me. "Why not?" My words were full of disbelief. With a subtle trace of accusation.

One of Dad's hands crept up to scratch the back of his neck. "It was sporadic. Limited. Some days it worked, some days it didn't. I didn't want to get your hopes up. And of course I didn't communicate with anyone at first."

The accusation went from a trace to full blown. "At first?"

"About a year ago, I did get in touch with another survivor. A music-label mogul from L.A., has a shelter in a remote area of Canada. He prepared in much the same way I did. His kids were older when they went in and he offered to send some of their music for you. So I downloaded it."

I pushed back my hair as I tried to sort the new information. "That's it? The Internet comes back up and you download music?"

Dad scrunched up his forehead. "Mmm, noooo. Things are slowly coming back out there. Of course most of the satellites would still have to be intact. I'm thinking a government somewhere, maybe ours, spread wireless Internet like a blanket, so survivors could be in contact with one another. Remember that place we went to in Colorado, on our skiing vacation?"

I nodded. "Yeah. They had free wireless all over town."

He laid his hands out toward me, like he was giving me a gift. "There you go, just like that."

It seemed so simple. Too simple. "So what else have you found out?"

Dad crossed his arms. "Not much, as far as conditions and such. I'm hopeful, if it was the government who got the Internet going again, that they'll start giving us updates."

"What about the phone? Does it work, too?"

Dad frowned. He shrugged slightly. "I try it now and then."

I sat up straighter, faced my father. I was nearly breathless. "Why can't we go outside now, and see? See what it's like out there?"

"Eli, you know what it's like out there."

"Dad, it's been years." I knew I was on the losing side of the debate due to the grim reality of radiation sickness; vile beyond belief, endless puke and diarrhea until you die. Oppenheimer's cholera.

"Eli, think about who you're talking to. I *do* know what it's like out there. And we've got to follow the plan if we have a chance of survival. The day will come when we open the door."

"How?"

"How what?"

Fists formed at my sides. I fought the urge to shout the words. "The door. How does it open?"

"There's a time lock, set to open fifteen years from the date we entered."

I already knew that much. Why was he so damned stingy with the details? I couldn't stop myself from asking, "Can it be opened before then?"

Dad scratched the stubble on his chin. "Oh, it can. With the code."

Even though I could assume the answer, I asked anyway. "Who knows the code?"

"I do, of course."

"Does Mom?"

His lip curled a bit. "I couldn't risk that. I didn't want you to know this, but a few months before we came down here she was having some problems."

This was news to me. "What kind of problems?"

"She was having some panic attacks, extreme anxiety. You were young, and you and your brother and sisters couldn't have understood that I had access to information about . . . things."

"What kind of things?"

"Government information. Mainly the probability of a nuclear attack."

"But you told Mom?"

He nodded. "She had to be medicated. And she can't be on antianxiety meds when she's pregnant. Her first bout of anxiety down here and she'd be running for the door, condemning us all."

I could see Dad's having ties to the government, but the stuff about Mom was bull. I didn't buy it at all. She was mostly calm and functional, especially given everything she'd gone through the past six years. My head started to hurt. I took a moment to rub my eyes. "So you're the only person who knows the code."

Dad took a big swig from a light blue bottle of antacid. It gave him a white mustache. He wiped it off with his sleeve. "Eli, I know what you're thinking. If nothing else, we're safe down here."

I met his gaze. "Can the door be opened from the outside?"

"No. Only inside. No one looking for it would ever find it, anyway." His expression became smug.

The smugness creeped me out. Just my opinion, but people in shelters after nuclear wars have no business being smug. "Why not?"

His hand moved up to scratch his head. "Remember what the land out there looks like?"

From what I could recall, the area was pretty but nondescript, with hills, trees. "Fairly basic landscape."

"For seven years, workers built this place. For seven years, they traveled forty miles from the closest town, past the stand of pine trees, went a mile, and took a left at a boulder. Then six more miles and several switchbacks in the road until they reached the shuttle."

"Shuttle?" I tried to keep my voice neutral. The *scrsshh scrsshh* sound of his scratching drove me crazy.

His hand dropped, coming to a stop on his bottle of antacid. "A bus basically, which took them the rest of the way to the supply entrance. Which was nowhere near the hatch.

And of course, on the shuttle ride they were blindfolded."
He took another drink, and then resumed his noisy
scratching.

Chills crawled up my spine as a lock of hair slipped off
my ear and over one eye. "They knew they were working
for you?"

Dad laughed. "Of course not. My accountant took care
of everything. They all thought it was for a sultan from
the Middle East. Old Phil cooked up one heckuva story. The
day they finished, they sealed up the supply entrance. Then
they drove away for the last time. The next day the pine
trees and boulders and any other landmarks disappeared.
There's no chance they could ever find it again without the
GPS coordinates. I made certain they didn't have those."

"Why did it have to be so secret?"

Dad leaned back in his chair, his hands finally coming
to a rest behind his head. "Don't be naïve, Eli. People will
do anything to survive. Had people known about this place
there would have been crowds begging to get in. I couldn't
have that."

"What about the shuttle driver? Wouldn't he know how
to get here?"

His expression changed. I tried to read it as his eyes
darted around the room before fixing on me again. "In the
end, I made sure he'd be taken care of."

My brain tried to embrace everything I'd just heard. "So
I can go on the Internet?"

Dad's eyes narrowed. "It's been down lately."

He was lying.

The day before, sitting in the hall outside his office, I *had* been connected. Just didn't know it at the time. I couldn't call him out—tell him that I knew he was lying. Defying my father was not on my list of things to do.

To his face, anyway. Behind his back was another story.

"I'll let you know when you can go on." His head leaned toward his bank of flat-screen computer monitors. "These are the only computers connected anyway."

That's what he thought. I stood up. "You'll let me know when I can go on," I repeated.

He nodded, taking another drink of antacid. I stood up to leave.

"Eli." His gaze fixed on me so intensely it was almost like being touched. My skin started to crawl.

"Your mother and sisters would only get upset. Unnecessarily upset."

I needed to get out of there.

"Do you understand what I'm saying?" There was no emotion in his voice. My throat tightened. I could only nod.

I left, shutting the door, trying not to sprint down the hall to my room. So I wasn't imagining things. The Internet *was* back up. Maybe I could find out what was going on outside these walls. If Dad had kept that information from me, chances were he was keeping other things secret as well. And I intended to find out what those secrets were.

CHAPTER NINE

On my way to get some lunch, my mind whirled. Man, first the Internet is connected, and then Dad says it's not. He lied right to my face. And lying only came that easily when you did it a lot. So what else was he lying about?

Little Miss Perfect skipped down the hall toward me. "Eli, you want to come with me? See the—"

"Shut up." First my mom, now my little sister. Was Terese that stupid? "How can you *be* with them? Spend time with them?"

Her chin rose as her hands went to her hips. "Eli. Someone has to take care of them, Mom can't do it all. Lexie and I *have* to help."

I couldn't do anything but shake my head and walk away. When had the Supplements morphed into family members?

Even pondering it was distasteful. The Supplements

were already the cause of too much weirdness in our world. Like the short-lived experiment with Tea.

We weren't really drinking tea—we just called our snack time Tea, thanks to Terese and her obsession with everything British. In the early years underground, we snacked on milk and stale cookies. But real milk had died with the cows. The UHT milk lasted a long time, and the powdered milk until Year Four. Dad had counted too much on the cows.

Mistake #47.

One afternoon, Lexie and Terese sat down with me for our afternoon snack of milk and cookies. Mom usually mixed up the powdered milk and poured a glass for each of us. One of those old-fashioned juice glasses with the little flowers on it. I always guzzled mine down, rather than use it to wash down the cookies. For those two and a half seconds every day, I pretended that I was still in the old world, Els standing by to refill my glass with an icy gallon jug of Land O' Lakes 2 percent.

But that day Mom wasn't there. Dad was. And the glasses were already filled when he brought the tray to the table. As always, I chugged mine. It didn't taste like the powdered milk we usually had. It was strange. Not in a bad way. More like the leftover milk at the bottom of a bowl of Cheerios with sugar.

I stuffed a ginger snap in my mouth as Lexie and Terese took their time, sipping their milk after every few bites of cookie. Dad didn't join us. He just waited until we were finished, then cleared his throat. Without any great theatrics, he told us the powdered milk was gone. And where that day's milk had come from.

Mom had an electric breast pump, and like a cow, the more she pumped the more she produced. I was thirteen and Lexie was fifteen. Mom and Dad were still getting along. Dad called her his little Holstein, because as long as she ate well and got enough rest, she produced a lot of milk. Plenty for the Supplements.

And for us.

I gagged and leaned over toward the floor.

"What?" Lexie looked up at Dad. She looked as repulsed as I felt.

Dad shrugged. "You're all still young, growing. You need nutrients wherever you can get them. This milk has calories, vitamin D, folic acid . . ."

I tuned him out, not wanting to hear some lengthy explanation. Like the scientific facts would justify it all. Like we were all supposed to say, "Oh, Father, thank you *again* for saving us."

Yeah, right.

The next day, the glasses were waiting at our spots. I crossed my arms and sat there. But it wasn't like we had a choice when Dad put his mind to something. My protest was short-lived and in the end I believed I had no choice but to drink it and gag. Lexie and Terese, too. Until one day Dad wasn't there at Tea time. Mom silently set powdered milk in front of us, and we never had the other "tea" again.

That experience was just another thing in our new world we wouldn't have even considered in the old.

Like the Supplements.

No way in hell was I going to get to know them. Not if there was the remotest chance they would meet their intended fate.

In the kitchen, over a lunch of warm tortillas from a big batch Mom froze before the flour went bad and fresh salsa, I pulled out a swivel barstool at the counter a few feet away from Lexie. Her long hair was up, and her velour was pink. She picked at her food, ignoring me.

The need to feel normal overwhelmed me. My world seemed so turned on its end that I needed to get a grip. Bothering my sister might help. "You're pretty in pink."

Her face turned my way with a hint of a smile.

"No, wait. You're pretty *pathetic* in pink." I laughed.

Her placid expression became a sneer. "Screw you."

"What has you all cranky on this beautiful day?" I smeared salsa all over my tortilla.

She rolled her eyes. "Mom is just so smug."

I took a drink of water and slammed my glass on the counter. The smug thing again. Dad might be smug. Mom certainly wasn't.

Lexie read my mind. "*Hello.* She's smug."

"She's in a bomb shelter, for cripes' sake. What the hell does she have to be smug about?"

Lexie ripped her tortilla into little pieces. "Don't you get it? She has everything she wants. A husband who dotes on her. No worries."

My laughter was so instantaneous I almost choked. "No worries? Take a look around."

Lexie sipped her water. "You look. What do most mothers of teenagers worry about?"

I shrugged and stuffed half a tortilla in my mouth, displaying it for her.

"Gross." She shifted her gaze away from me. "They worry about their kids driving cars because they might be in an accident. They worry if they don't come home on time. Then there's drugs, alcohol, tons of crap—"

"What's your point, Lex?"

One of her hands slapped the counter. "She doesn't have to worry about any of it. Her kids are all here; her rich husband isn't going to run off with his secretary."

With part of a tortilla I scooped up some errant salsa. "You're forgetting the fact she's trapped underground with a husband who . . ." I'd never voiced the truth aloud. I didn't think I could.

"What?" Lexie had stopped eating to stare at me.

I shrugged.

"Come on, a husband who what? What were you going to say?"

"Nothing."

She turned to baby talk to taunt me. "Is widdo Ewi afwaid?"

I practically shouted the words. "A husband who breeds new kids to feed to his old ones."

Lexie's mouth dropped open.

I didn't even need to pause for effect. "There's a type of dinosaur that did the same thing." I snapped my fingers. "Hey, they could name it after Dad. The Yanakakasaurus."

Lexie glared at me. "How can you say that?"

I hadn't meant to. She pissed me off and it just slipped out.

Since it did, I kept going. "God, you are so clueless. He lies to us, all the time. Always has. At least Mom never lies. And I bet she would give anything to have us out in the world, even with all that. I think she would leave this place in a heartbeat."

Lexie bit her lip. "You're on her side."

She was really starting to ruin my lunch. "Last time I checked, we're all on the same side. The underside."

"*Hello*. Eli. We're not all on the same side." Lexie launched herself off the stool. "You think you're better than me, that you're smarter. In the old world you—" She stopped.

The look on her face made me curious. "What?"

She blew out a big breath. "You were such a brat. You never cared about anybody. You got away with it because you had Eddy. You had your own little wonderful world with your twin always there for you. You never knew what it was like to be lonely."

As I chewed, I thought about it. She wasn't wrong.

Her eyes narrowed. "You know what it was like for me?"

Some salsa dripped down my chin. I wiped it off with a paper napkin.

"Of course not, because you never cared enough to ask. At school, everyone was my friend because of who I was, how much money we had. I never really knew if any of my friends liked me for me. You never had to worry about that, because you always had Eddy."

I crumpled the napkin, dropping it on my plate. "Not anymore."

"Exactly." Her words were biting. "Poor Eli, now you're in the same boat as the rest of us. Guess what. You don't want to hear it, but you're like me. And me and you? We're just like Dad. We don't care about other people and we're only out for ourselves."

I pushed away my empty plate. "That's a load of bull."

"It's true, you know it. Terese is just like Mom. She's a weird little kid, but she cares about other people. Like Eddy did. That's why Mom and Terese allow themselves to love the Supplements. Because there is no way they would ever . . . ever . . . ever use them for their intended purpose." She paused. "But you and me? Hell no. I do my work there, and then leave. You stay away completely."

"Dad says it's women's work."

Her eyes narrowed. "Don't blame it on him."

I rolled my eyes. Then who was I supposed to blame?

"You stay away." She leaned closer. "Know why? Because you know, deep down, if it comes down to starving, we will . . . do what we need to do." She jabbed her finger in the air toward me. "The problem is you're deluded. You *think* you're with Mom and Terese on this one. You aren't. And the day will come when you have to pick a side." Lexie reached toward me.

I jumped back.

She laughed. "Freak." She turned on her heel and walked out, leaving her dishes.

She was wrong.

I hoped she was wrong, anyway. Wrong about me and Dad. Even if I was like Dad. He was brilliant. But was he a good man?

I picked up Lexie's dishes and put them in the dishwasher with mine. I wiped up some salsa that had spilled on the counter. Without all the kitchen staff we were used to, I'd learned to clean up after myself. Hated it at first, wondered why that couldn't be women's work, too, but I'd once read that it only takes twenty days to create a new habit. And I'd had way more than that to change my ways.

Dad came in, holding a book and awkwardly scratching his right arm. "You already have lunch?"

"Yeah."

Dad sat down and started to read. He looked as if he'd be there for a while.

I hoped so. I wanted to see if the Internet was up. I stopped by my room to grab Eddy's laptop. I jogged over to Dad's office. I sat down in the hallway cross-legged, and hit the laptop's power button. I tapped my leg with the back of my hand. *Come on, come on.*

And there it was.

Wireless Network Not Available.

"What? No. No. No." I was right next to the office door. Same spot I was the last time. What was different?

Dad. The last time Dad had been in his office.

Did he only have it flipped on when he was in there?

Just in case someone wandered down the hall with a laptop?

I sat up straight.

That was exactly it.

He couldn't keep the wireless signal from going out in the hall. It was easier to keep people out of the hall.

And easier still to keep Internet capability off of the computers.

My hands tightened on the laptop, which had just become the most crucial item in my possession.

Until I got a chance to connect to the Internet, until I knew what was really going on, one thing was for sure. I would have to keep my dad from finding it.

CHAPTER **TEN**

THAT NIGHT I DREAMED OF TURDUCKENS. SUCCULENT ROWS of them, lined up side by side on the banquet table in the ballroom in our Seattle house.

The glowing amber digits on my clock proclaimed 4:13 A.M. when I woke up, my appetite tortured. Lying there and reminiscing made it a thousand times worse. But it felt impossible to move as the memory rushed back.

Eddy and I were nine. Dad ordered a dozen turduckens to feed the guests at our annual Christmas Eve dinner. Christmas mornings were just for family. But the night before was reserved for the hordes of people Dad had worked with over the year. And, being a Rex Yanakakis shindig, the main course had to be something unusual. No run-of-the-mill turkey or ham or goose for my father.

So turduckens it was.

What is a turducken? An exclusive culinary creation available by special order from some little Cajun town down South. Entirely deboned, a turducken consists of a turkey, stuffed with a duck, stuffed with a chicken, like an edible Russian nesting doll. Some were stuffed with alligator, crab, shrimp; my favorite was the traditional cornbread variety.

That Christmas Eve, Dad oversaw the kitchen staff himself, making sure everything was perfect. Dressed in tuxedos, Eddy and I stood at the door along with Lexie, who wore a floor-length green velvet dress. With practiced smiles on our faces, we stood there, waiting to greet the guests. We heard the vehicles as they drove in, idling near the front door while the valets hired for the evening helped the guests out before relieving them of their cars.

The guests entered through an awning and red carpet set up for the evening. After they gushed over us for a moment or two, they handed off their coats to the servants. Then they were checked off the list which, I suspected, read like a who's who of anyone of any technological and scientific importance within a hundred-mile radius of the Space Needle. My mom loved causes, especially the ones that aimed to save the environment or children in developing countries, and was on the board of many charitable organizations. So the other half of the list most likely was a who's who of prominent local activists.

With all the activists and scientists, many of whom were probably animal-rights people, there must have been plenty of vegetarians in the room. There was no way to tell simply by looking which faction any of them might have belonged to. This was the party of the season, and everyone was in tuxes or long evening wear, mingling around, holding their drinks until a tinkling bell signaled it was time to gather around the overflowing buffet table.

The three of us lined up next to Mom, who wore a red velvet ball gown and held Terese, who wore a smaller version. First Dad made a short speech, thanking everyone for being there. Kind of pointless, in my opinion, since people would have paid good money to attend that function.

The tradition held that Dad was to carve and present the first few servings. So, as Dad sliced with a flourish into the turducken, revealing the layers of varying shades of poultry, the room was still. Except for the enthusiastic and merry orchestra playing "I'll Be Home for Christmas."

The smells of the trinity of poultry mingled with the rest of the feast, creating a tantalizing aroma. Thinking about it so many years later, I had to smile as I thought about what might have been going through people's heads as they lined up.

The people who didn't eat meat wondered how to get out of partaking in what was obviously the pièce de résistance of the Rex Yanakakis Christmas Eve Dinner.

The animal-rights people cringed, not wanting to voice their objections for fear of pissing off Clea Sheridan Yanakakis, who was very generous to their causes with her husband's money.

The people who did eat meat tried to ignore the jittery noncarnivores surrounding them.

In his black Armani tuxedo, Dad set the first slice of turducken on one of the expensive china plates in a tall stack beside him and held it up. "Get a plate from me and you can pile on the rest of the buffet. Who's first?"

He passed out the plates. Murmurs arose until the noise level was back to normal. From my place beside Mom, I glanced around the room as people ate, most avoiding the 430-calorie serving of striated poultry resting in an ominous fashion on their plates. Then, after that first turducken was served, Dad started making the rounds. I watched him make small talk, perhaps asking if they tried the turducken yet. He'd wait while each guest had eaten at least one bite in front of him, ever the dutiful host, making sure his guests were taken care of.

After everyone had been served, the Yanakakis children were ushered upstairs where we changed into pajamas and ate our own turducken dinner. Eddy and I loved the stuff. Grumpy Els brought two huge pieces up to our TV room. Rich and flavorful, turducken was perfect for making Christmas Eve dinner memorable.

Like every year when we'd finished eating, Eddy and I hid in the library, the one room in our mansion where guests thought they could escape to, unnoticed. Eddy and I had learned that during parties the library was where we were most likely to spy someone saying or doing something . . . well . . . *interesting*.

Our social life was sheltered, to say the least. Rare were the moments when we were allowed to go somewhere on our own, without supervision. We lived for the unpredictable moments that Dad's dinner guests usually provided.

His belly full like mine, Eddy actually fell asleep in our

hiding spot in one of the long storage seats along the window. We'd stuffed pillows in for comfort, too much so in Eddy's case. Though the music was muffled from my vantage point, I heard the orchestra move on to traditional carols.

I stayed awake by humming along softly with the songs I knew. During "Hark! the Herald Angels Sing," someone came in the library. I lifted the cover to hear better, trying not to make any noise.

I immediately recognized the man by his voice: Dad's accountant, Phil. He was with a woman.

She groaned. "I ate too much, this dress is tight now."

"Stupid turducken."

I heard sloppy sounds.

The woman spoke again. "Do you think Rex realized how many vegetarians had their first bite of meat in like, decades, tonight? I can't believe no one just flat out refused."

"They could have just said no."

"How do you refuse Rex Yanakakis? Especially when he's standing right there."

Phil's voice was a growl. "He loves that."

"What do you mean?"

"The meat. He knew half the guests were vegetarian or vegan or PETA. It was a game."

"A game?"

"Oh yeah. The let's-see-what-I-can-get-them-to-do-just-because-I'm-Rex-Yanakakis game."

"He said that?"

Phil laughed. "Of course not. It's always like this with him. He won't brag or use his name to get preferential treatment, but once in a while, he has to test his power to see how far his name and money and reputation will go. Or how far they'll get someone else to go."

The woman's dress rustled. "He does so much good with his money."

"Exactly. Which is why he can get away with this. That's why we all let him get away with it."

"I can't believe he would think that way."

Phil chuckled. "If Rex is anything, it's calculating. His whole life is planned. When he was eighteen, he lost out on a prestigious fellowship to a Chinese girl. Of course, by that time his parents were dead and he had plenty of money for school. It still irked him. He told me he swore at the time it would never happen to any kids of his. So what's he do? Marries a hot Chinese chick."

"I thought she was Hawaiian."

"Yeah, she's Chinese, too. He sends those twins of his to Chinese school."

There were more sounds, smooching.

She spoke again. "So what do you do for him? I mean, any company secrets you can share?"

"Oh, I'm working on something big."

"What?" She squealed.

"I could tell you, but then I'd have to kill you." Phil pushed out a contented sigh. "Let's just say I'm going to retire a very wealthy man."

The orchestra began a slow, beautiful rendition of "O

Holy Night." Goose bumps rose on my arms. Suddenly my stomach stuffed with the turkey stuffed with a duck stuffed with a chicken was not as settled as previously thought. I shoved the bench cover as far as it would go, springing up and out, racing past the two adults. They were locked tight in an embrace, and if they noticed me slipping by them, they didn't let on.

I tried to make it to the bathroom, but my foot caught on the hallway carpet. I tripped, landing on the floor in time to spew my guts on the shoes in front of me—white orthopedic oxfords that belonged to Els.

I hadn't thought about that night for a long time. Maybe I'd forgotten it.

Well, until that moment after the turducken dream. The memory of that Christmas Eve was so clear, like it had just happened. That totally sucked to hear Phil say those things about my dad. I was eight. Dad was my hero. I thought he was everyone else's, too. I never doubted it before that night.

But thinking about that night, about Phil, I made a connection. How deeply was he involved in the Compound and the secrecy surrounding it? How far had he gone to keep it a secret?

I tossed and turned, my heart pounding. I must have drifted back to sleep at some point, because the next thing I knew I awoke to warm hands on my face, slapping sweetly.

I tried to see through my grogginess and my hair as my hands automatically formed a shield.

Terese giggled.

My eyes snapped into focus. A blond-haired cherub sat on my chest, gurgling as it smacked me again.

One of the Supplements.

What the—!

"Reese!" I sat up and pushed the thing off me. "Get out of here!" I tried to jump out of bed, but my legs were entangled in the sheets. I only succeeded in falling onto the floor, dragging most of the bedding with me. "Get out!"

"Calm down. He's just a child." Terese bounced the Supplement in her arms. "Quinn, can you say 'Eli'?"

"Get out of here!" I yelled, throwing pillows at her, hard, until I drove them out of my room. I kicked free of my covers and lunged for the door, slamming it behind them.

My legs shook too hard to hold me. I collapsed against the wall, my hair covering my face.

My breath came too fast.

My heartbeat skipped.

Sweat broke out on my forehead.

One of the Supplements had touched me.

For six years, no one had touched me, skin on skin.

Little Miss Perfect didn't understand. She didn't understand how our circumstances would deteriorate; forcing us to do things no one should ever have to do. Things necessary for our survival. Things that would become impossible to carry out if we ever came to care for the Supplements.

With both hands, I smoothed my hair back from my

face, holding it there for a moment as I tried to compose myself.

Still trembling, I walked into the bathroom and didn't get in the shower until it was steaming hot. I wanted the fragrant soap and the flowing water to wash away the unwelcome touch, the dream, the memory of that long ago Christmas party—everything.

It didn't work. Because no matter how I tried, I couldn't erase how fresh and soft those little hands had been on my face. I refused to let myself dwell on how exquisite that warm, innocent touch had felt.

A touch like that was meant for someone good.

For someone who deserved it.

A touch like that was not meant for someone like me.

CHAPTER ELEVEN

THAT MORNING WAS ONE WE HAD MUSIC. MOM HAD BEEN giving us lessons since we were little. Lexie played piano, so with Terese's oboe, my trumpet, and Mom's cello, we played a lot of group pieces. We weren't a string quartet, but Mom created her own arrangements for us, based on many classic ones.

We had been working on her variation of Beethoven's String Quartet no. 15 in A Minor. Mom led us off, the deep tone of the cello setting an eerie aura. Each of us was to join one by one, almost in a fugal pattern, as we gradually repeated the melody in succession. There were leading tones on the strong beat, and then there were quiet, slower half notes that felt mysterious, almost sinister.

Not a picker upper, by any means.

My trumpet took the violin's part, which had a difficult entrance of running sixteenth notes. I took a breath, pressed my lips to the silver mouthpiece, and began.

Lexie slammed her hands on the keys, the sound loud and discordant. "God, Eli. You were frickin' late!"

I took my lips away from the mouthpiece. "Was not."

Mom kept playing. "Watch your language, Lexie. You're both doing fine; let's pick it up where we are. Come on."

Lexie groaned. She started playing again.

Terese and I joined in. Terese's oboe played the part of the bass, and the rest of us played in opposition to her. The intensity, and volume, grew as we moved through the piece. We were good.

The piece was long, but we had no more interruptions or mistakes. As it came to a close, the harmony strengthened and progressed to the simple ending, which was a solo for me with accompanying chords from Lexie. At least our instruments cooperated, no small feat considering Lexie's clenched jaw and drilling stare.

For a few moments, I felt like we belonged together, like we had bonded through the music if not through circumstance. At the end of the session, we put our instruments away in silence. Lexie stormed away quickly, while Mom fiddled with the latch on the cello case, distracted. Terese just smiled to herself and didn't make eye contact with me.

My palms were sweaty and my stomach felt queasy. Music was supposed to be soothing. Like most of our music days, I found myself grasping my trumpet, taking my time as I shined it before putting it back into its case. Despite the discordance, I was reluctant to end the session. But with a click, the case closed and I was back to feeling alone.

In the middle of the afternoon, Dad came into the

library where I was reading. "I'm working on inventory and I need you to help," he announced flatly.

Inventory sucked.

I tossed Stephen King onto one of the leather chairs.

Dad sent me to one of the larger storage rooms and left me on my own with a yellow legal pad and a pen. Everything had to be accounted for. Every jar of pickles. Every bottle of laundry detergent. Every box of feminine hygiene products. Lovely.

The task took me about three hours, filled several pages, and yielded few surprises. For five years I'd done this chore, dutifully following my father's orders. I'd watched the piles of jars, bottles, and boxes slowly shrink. Not to emergency levels, but still.

When I came to the boxes of cleaning supplies, our least necessary inventory in my opinion, I noticed an opening at the back, between stacks of paper towels and cartons of toilet paper. No clue why I bothered moving them aside. Before I'd always just estimated by the height of the stack. But as I shifted them for the first time ever, there was a plastic tub that seemed out of place with all the cardboard containers around it.

I lugged it down from the shelf and read the one word written in black Sharpie on the blue cover:

Eddy

My knees buckled. I dropped to the floor. With one trembling finger I traced the letters. I hadn't seen his name in writing for so long, hadn't thought of him for a few hours. Seeing those letters together, so familiar and heart-breaking at the same time . . .

I tore off the cover.

Plastic bags of Jack Link's. Lots of them. Beef jerky, turkey jerky, sausage sticks. Eddy's favorite food on earth. I ripped open a bag of jerky and stuck my nose deep inside. I breathed in the one scent that could bring my brother alive to me. Inside the storage closet, I remained on the cement floor for a long time, inhaling my twin.

My stomach rumbled. It occurred to me I might be holding an important find. The wrapper crinkled as I bit off a hunk of jerky.

A bit past its prime. But still tasty. Still meat.

I downed two-thirds of a bag before replacing the top of the tub. I carried it into the kitchen. Terese sat at the counter. Mom sliced tomatoes for a salad.

Despite the deep circles under her eyes and slumped shoulders, Mom smiled when she saw the look on my face. "What's that?"

My hands guided the box onto the counter. I slid onto a stool.

Terese read the cover. "Eddy's box?"

At one time, we all had a box, a box filled with our favorite treat. Snickers for me, plain M&M's for Terese, coffee-flavored Nips for Mom, Corn Nuts for Dad. I didn't know what Lexie's was. She never ate junk food at home, but she must have had a box, too.

Mom lifted the cover and laughed. Her eyes lit up for

the first time in a while. "I hated this stuff. It smelled so greasy and smoky. He always reeked of it."

I held up a bag. "It's meat."

Mom's brow furrowed. "It's still good? I don't want anyone getting sick."

The ingredients list didn't indicate much. "I'm not sure it was ever good." Yet moments before, chewing the jerky, I'd tasted the saltiness, felt the weight of it, the substance that vegetables and other foods lacked. "Yeah, it's still edible." I realized how much I missed meat.

"But it belongs to Eddy." Little Miss Perfect looked from me to Mom.

Mom smiled at Terese. "Lovey, I don't think Eddy would mind."

Terese opened a bag. She gnawed off a chunk of jerky. "Rather difficult to chew."

Mom reached for a piece.

Together, they chewed the jerky. Sloppy and loud.

"It's not so bad." Mom went back to making a salad.

Terese picked an unopened bag out of the box and ran from the room.

I told Mom, "Be right back." There was a little business I had to take care of. In the hall, I caught up to Terese and grabbed her by her hood, yanking her back. "How'd you get in my room?"

Her mouth was full and she finished chewing as she tried to wrestle away from me. "Opened the door."

I gripped harder and pulled, so that she was bent over backward looking up at me.

"You can't have just opened the door, it was locked."

"Ow, let go!" She put a hand on the wall to keep her balance.

"Tell me how you got in."

She rolled her eyes. "I read *Oliver Twist*."

"Say what? And he picks locks?"

She twisted as far as she could to one side, but I had such a tight hold of her hood, she only succeeded in almost strangling herself. She huffed. "Not exactly. But it got me interested, so I found a book in the library."

I shook my head. "On how to pick locks." You'd think I might have found that one at some point.

She spoke fast, probably figuring I'd let her go as soon as she told me everything. "It was that one for kids that shows how everything is made. It tells how things work and I learned about locks and figured it out."

I let her go and stepped back, leaning against the wall. I lowered my voice. "So what other locks have you picked down here?"

She stuck out her tongue as she skipped backward, away from me. "I'm not telling you!" And she ran off down the hall.

I went back in the kitchen. "She's such a little freak."

Mom shook a finger at me. "You shouldn't say that about her. And I think she's better now that she moved in . . ." She trailed off, like she didn't mean to say the words.

"Moved in where?"

"The yellow room."

"Mom! How could you let her do that?"

Her eyes narrowed. "Watch your tone. And she spends so much time in there, anyway. I didn't see any harm."

"Whatever. I just miss everyone being normal." Then I smiled and tried to make light. "Actually I miss a lot of things."

Mom sighed. "I miss . . . ," she hesitated, her eyes on the wilting lettuce. "I would give anything for a huge, whole milk, four-pump latte right now, with loads of caramel sauce." She shrugged and went back to the salad.

I watched her for a bit. Her shoulders seemed slumped and her movements were mechanical, almost robotic.

"Mom," I ventured, "you happy?"

She paused, staring into the salad bowl. "Happy? I'm alive. Warm. Reasonably fed. My family, most of it, is here with me." Her eyes met mine. "I never dreamed I could be this miserable ever. Don't get me wrong, I'm grateful. Grateful that my husband went to all this trouble . . ."

I saw the question in her eyes at the same time I felt it in my gut. "What are we surviving for?" I asked.

She nodded. "Did we survive simply for the sake of surviving? The rest of our lives, we just exist to survive?"

Tears welled up as she set a hand on her stomach. "I wanted so much for my children. For a while you had it all. Good schools, everything you could want to make a great childhood. And I was happy. Down here, though . . ." She took a deep breath and let it out. Her voice had a slight quiver to it. "You are all so affected by this place in your own ways."

My first inclination was to disagree and I started to protest.

Her expression shut me up. "Don't deny it, Eli. I want us to thrive again. But this isn't it. It isn't even close." Her hands went up to cover her face as her shoulders shook.

I just sat there. Sat there and watched her weep.

Part of me wanted to hold her. All of me knew that's what a good son would do.

Alas, I fell neatly into the category of lousy son.

I snatched some napkins off the counter and set them down next to her.

"Thanks." She wiped her eyes, then blew her nose. "You know your father and I aren't . . . sharing a room anymore."

I thought of the couch in Dad's office, the pillow and blanket. Not like we had a guest room for him to retreat to. But I didn't want her to know I'd noticed anything. "Since when?"

"For a while. We don't agree on a few things." She patted her belly.

It was pretty clear to me that the gesture referred to the Supplements. They meant only one thing to my father, yet clearly they were something else entirely to my mother. And all that time I had been suffering from the delusion that I could remain uninvolved, choosing to side with neither of them.

I put both my elbows on the counter and rested my chin on my hands. "Mom, if you could leave here, would you?"

She wiped her eyes again. "Only if it didn't put any of you in danger."

"You just said you want us to thrive."

She nodded. "Yes. I do. But I also want you alive. And if surviving is all we can have at this point, I guess I just have to live with that."

I sat back up. My fingers pulled at the collar of my T-shirt. "Do you think things are really like Dad says?"

She peeked in the oven door. "I have no way of knowing."

I had expected her to reassure me, tell me that Dad knew what he was doing like he always did. But her answer gave me an opening, an opening to see if I could trust her. And I needed to trust her.

I swallowed. "Did he tell you the Internet is up?"

Mom grabbed the edge of the oven to steady herself. "What?" Her surprise was definitely genuine.

"I take it that's a no." I told her what Dad had told me.

She sat down. Her face was pale. "You know, my mother never wanted me to marry your father."

"Why not?"

She'd never talked to me this way before. Like an adult.

"Oh, where should I start? He was such a complete package, you know. Smart, good-looking, rich. I usually liked taller men. But, you know, I figured he could always stand on his wallet." She grinned, but it looked uncomfortable.

My forced laugh felt the same way.

She shrugged a bit. "Your gram just didn't trust him. She said he seemed too controlling. All I saw was a man who could make my dreams, and the dreams of my future children, come true." She paused.

I really didn't want to hear any more. Despite everything, that had always been a constant for me. Something to draw strength from. My parents and the life they made together. Not perfect, but strong nonetheless. It was not pleasant to find out the foundation of your house had dry rot.

She continued, "And he was so involved with the orphanage. He never hesitated when I saw Lexie and knew I had to take her home with us. I knew my kids would never want for anything. I know it might sound shallow to you, Eli. But it was such a relief to know I was marrying a man I wouldn't have to fight over money with."

It was my turn to say something. All I could come up with was "And now?"

The oven's timer buzzed.

Mom stood, pulling on her thick red oven mitts. "I honestly don't know."

I watched Mom pull a loaf of flat bread out of the oven. She chewed on the inside of one cheek, distorting her face. As she set the hot fresh bread on the cooling rack, the funny-smelling bread that no one but Dad would eat, I could tell what was running through her mind.

Dad came in then, sat beside me and asked for my inventory sheets. He scanned the page, and then scratched his neck. "I'm not sure where I miscalculated, but my last figures were off."

Mom must have decided it was a good time to start talking to him again. "Is this where you tell us when the food will run out?" Her voice was full of worry, yet there was also a harsh tone to it.

Dad didn't even notice. His finger trailed down a paper on his clipboard. "About a year before the fifteen years are up. Depending on the hydroponics, of course."

He could have been giving us the weather report.

Mom tapped the knife on the cutting board. "The vegetables will last. We'll have enough food."

I spoke up. "Why can't we just be vegetarians?"

Dad laughed a little as he dropped his pen on the clipboard and shoved it aside. "They rely on eggs and dairy products for protein."

"What about vegans? They don't eat any animal products, do they?"

Mom answered me. "Because they have soy products and nuts for protein. Your father was never a fan of soy and the nuts are long gone."

Dad leaned his head to one side as he looked at her. He stood up and walked over to the counter. He sliced off a piece of bread and tossed it between his hands to cool. "By my calculations, protein will be totally lacking. We won't have a choice."

Mom snapped at him. "There's always a choice."

"Of course there's a choice. Do you want to live or die?" He held out the bread to me. "Bread?"

"No!" Mom's face fell as she looked from Dad to the bread. "I mean, there's another loaf for the kids. Still baking." She gestured at the oven. "This one's all yours."

Dad smiled. "Thanks." He bit into the bread.

My head started to hurt.

Dad shifted his gaze to Mom. "Yes, there's always a

chance we won't have to go to extreme measures. But we won't know until that time and we need to set ourselves up now. We must do what we can. We need to bolster our supplemental food supply."

She glared at him. "Unless you've come up with something to guarantee multiple births, I'm already working at my quota." But the look on her face showed she regretted her words.

He cut another slice. "Eli, come with me."

Mom shook her head. "Don't do this, Rex."

His voice was low. "Eli, let's go."

She dropped the knife on the counter and watched us leave.

What was going on?

Dad walked slightly in front of me as we headed toward the direction of his office. "Eli, I'm going to need your help." Both his hands started to scratch his face.

All that scratching was uncomfortable for me to watch. And it was making me itchy again. I wanted to grab his hands, make him stop. But I couldn't. Instead, I looked down at my feet. "With what?"

"Your mother and I can only, well, work so fast, so to speak."

My stomach lurched. "What am I supposed to do?"

He cleared his throat. "There are other ways to . . . enhance our food supply."

I didn't know where his reasoning was headed. Or maybe I didn't want to admit it. My mind was so clouded that I missed his next few words.

Dad kept on. "It would be a true experiment, since no one has done it before. But think, if I could pull it off . . ." He grinned. "I could patent the process and it could be used for generations. It would revolutionize medicine. People in need of organ transplants wouldn't have to wait. And—"

"I missed what you said. What would revolutionize medicine?"

We reached his office and he unlocked it, ushering me in. Then he walked over to the padlocked door and pulled a key out of his pocket. With a twist, he had the padlock off and his hand was on the knob. "Are you ready?"

As the door swung open, my first impression was a glare of white light. When I stepped inside, I realized it was the whiteness of the room enhanced by the fluorescent bulbs running everywhere overhead. The room was a laboratory, so full of equipment and so big, that it made the other lab look like a low-budget high school classroom.

My jaw dropped as I took a few steps farther in. After all this time, a part of our world that I had no idea existed.

Long white counters ran hundreds of yards in front of me, each lined with test tubes and beakers and enormous, intimidating microscopes. Along the walls sat machines I'd never seen before. A lump formed in my throat. "Dad? What do you do in here? What would revolutionize medicine?"

His tone was matter of fact. "Cloning a human being."

I backed away from him. The words almost didn't make it out of my mouth. "What in the world are you proposing?"

Dad picked up a test tube and peered at the substance inside. He jotted something on a nearby clipboard. "We've been doing it the old-fashioned way. We need to step it up and make more Supplements the new-fangled way."

I retched, barely making it to a sink before I puked up all the jerky. As the faucet went full blast, I lifted up the bottom of my T-shirt and wiped my face. My back was to him. "You can't mean that."

He grunted, annoyed, "Come on, Eli."

I whirled to face him again. "It goes against nature! You know that. Besides, none of those animal clones lived more than a short time."

Dad tilted his head a bit, looking at me. "Eli, Eli, Eli. When are you going to realize you're just like me? Eddy isn't . . . wasn't, not by a long shot. But you? You are. You'll do whatever it takes, anything, to make sure you come out on top."

"That's not true!" His analysis was akin to that clown's telling me I was the evil twin. My head hurt behind my left eye and my vision started to blur.

He nodded. "Yeah, it is. You can't deny what you are."

My head moved from side to side. "I won't do it. You can't make me help you."

He sighed. "No, I can't. You're right." He drummed his fingers on the counter.

Dad seemed like he'd actually listened to me.

So I offered up an olive branch. "It's just weird, you know?" I gestured at the scene around me. "Cloning people. And besides, don't you need a human host at some point? And Mom's already got a tenant, so to speak."

Dad shrugged a bit. "There's Lexie."

Was he insane? "I know Lexie. She won't do it."

He chuckled a bit. "Do you? Do you really know your sister?"

Oh God. No. I probably didn't.

He set the test tube down and picked up another. "I've already spoken to Lexie. She's waiting for you to get on board."

I turned, heading out the door and through his office, making it to the corridor mere seconds before I broke down.

Harsh sobs racked my body as I leaned on a wall. Was this what our life had become?

I hadn't ever loved life in here. Tolerated it, maybe. But hearing my father's plan for our continued survival caused a major shift inside of me. Any lingering tolerance, any sliver of ambivalence had fled. Gone for good. The space they left in me abruptly filled with hate for everything about the Compound.

I refused to live that way. There wasn't anything I could do about it by myself. Maybe it *was* time to take sides.

I hoped I could find someone to be on mine.

CHAPTER TWELVE

I CALMED MYSELF DOWN, CLEANED MYSELF UP, AND HOLED up in my room. I stayed there the rest of the day. Even skipped dinner. I didn't want to see anyone. But I wanted to pick up my book from the library.

As I left my room, I almost tripped over Mom, who was sitting on the floor, her back against the hard wall. I got the feeling she'd been waiting for me. I wondered how much she had heard of my earlier argument with Dad. Or how much she perhaps already knew.

She looked up at me with gentle, wet eyes. "Eli, come see the babies with me."

My face must have given away my reaction.

She held out a hand for me to help her up, then pulled back when I did. "I have stood by and watched your father do a lot of things," she said, inching up the wall. "But this—I won't give in."

Her tone told me what I had to do. I went to meet the rest of the family.

How could I possibly have gone that long without seeing them? We were, after all, stuck in the Compound together. But it was a big place. Big enough to be able to avoid what I needed to avoid. But maybe I'd avoided enough: facing life without Eddy and Gram, surviving the worst disaster to hit the civilized world. Hell, I'd become a master at denial.

Then Mom led me into the room with the yellow door.

My first look around made me realize the depth of my father's preparation for any contingency. Goose bumps covered my arms. I resisted the urge to let my hair down and hide from the truth.

The walls were sunflower yellow, dotted here and there with painted handprints of pleasing greens and blues and oranges. The tone of the lighting was artificial sunlight. Did I imagine my skin becoming warmer? I felt like I was outside on a warm April afternoon. The scent of lilacs lingered, increasing the sensation of spring.

There was a crib and two toddler beds, all oak, with fluffy down bedding in whimsical, primary-colored prints. On the floor beside them lay a mattress, topped with a twisted mess of sheets and blankets. Past the beds, into the second room of the suite, we entered the playroom. Castles of blocks were stacked against one wall, and another held shelves brimming with picture books, puzzles, and games.

My eyes widened at the amount of baby and toddler things my father had stockpiled.

Had Dad planned on Mom having babies here? Before the Compound, I never heard them discuss having more children. Everything in that room suggested otherwise. And when I saw the stacks of diapers, the changing table, and the rocking chair I realized this had all been foreseen by my father somehow.

Maybe foreseen wasn't the right word. Maybe he'd always planned to create a new generation.

Someone took my hand.

I recoiled, yanking it away. A small, dark-haired boy dressed in navy blue sweats grinned up at me. I recognized the fabric was from the piles of bolts in the sewing room.

His face was also one I knew well. Eddy's. My legs nearly buckled and I put a hand against the wall to steady myself.

He still looked up at me. "Want to play Chutes and Ladders?"

Terese stood behind him. "Eli, this is Lucas."

"Do you want to play with me, Eli?"

I wanted to shout no and run. But where?

Mom said, "I'll come by in a little while." She backed out the door.

Part of me was so pissed at her, for going along with all this. But another part of me was too surprised at the new world I'd stepped into. I was jolted by how much the little boy resembled Eddy at that age. And me.

A brother. I had another brother.

The boy must have equated my silence with agreement, because he walked over to a table with small chairs where a game was set up. He tapped one place. "You sit here, 'kay?"

I tried to sit where he directed, but could hardly get my legs under the tiny table. I moved the chair and sat on the floor.

He sat in a chair beside me, his eyes level with mine. "I go first, 'kay?" He counted the spaces and moved his piece.

Curious fascination overcame the knot in my stomach. "How high can you count?"

"I can count a lot. I'm almost five."

I took my turn. "Figured you were."

We kept playing. The boy, Lucas, chattered the whole time, telling me about what he liked to play. At one point he stopped and rested his chin on one hand. His big brown eyes contemplated my face. "You look like me."

My laughter came before I could stop it. "I was here first, so that means *you* look like *me*."

"And Eddy."

I felt my smile collapse. "How do you know about Eddy?" I glanced around for Terese, but didn't see her.

"Reesie told me. About Eddy and Eli, the twins. Eddy stayed outside to take care of Cocoa and Clementine. He's going to come and get us out."

Lucas knew no life besides the Compound. Yet even he felt the need to get out. If that didn't signify the strangeness of our life, I don't know what would.

Guess it was up to me to shatter his illusions. "Look, kid. Eddy isn't out there. He's gone."

The statement didn't seem to unsettle him at all. He simply looked at me. And he sounded very confident. "Reesie said you'd say that."

I had no response.

"Why didn't you come see me before?"

"Before what?"

"Now." Lucas blinked. His dark lashes were a stark contrast to his pale, perfect skin. Such a beautiful child.

Again, I didn't have anything to say.

Then he handed me a toy car. "It's broken."

"Huh?"

"It's broken. Can you fick it?"

His face was so serious. I couldn't help but laugh. "Yeah, I can fick it." The wheel had come off. I pried it back on.

As he leaned in to watch me, he was close, so close that I could feel his warm breath on my arm.

Too close.

My body tensed, waiting for my heart to speed up, my breath to become shallow. But it didn't happen.

I finished, handing back his toy.

Lucas smiled. "Thanks." He dropped to the floor, running the car back and forth until he seemed satisfied it worked. He checked behind him, and then whispered, "Eli, can you keep a secret?"

"Yeah, of course." Like there was anyone to tell.

Lucas led me over to a door. Inside, shelves upon shelves held toys, puzzles, and games. He went to the back, tugging out a wooden box. "I keep this back here so no one else can see it. It's special." He beckoned.

With one hand, he selected an item from the box. His grin showed a lot of teeth. "Look." He held up a painted figure of an intricately carved clown.

Great. It had to be a clown.

He removed the top, which revealed another smaller figure inside the first.

"Oh, they're nesting dolls."

Lucas scrunched his nose up. "They're not dolls. They were a special present. A secret." He plucked one out of the other until there were six. He set them on a shelf in order, keeping the smallest in his hand. "This is the last one." He held a finger to his lips. "It has a mystery inside."

"The last one doesn't open, that *is* the mystery."

Lucas nodded. "It does so have a mystery."

Was I actually arguing with a four-year-old? "Okay, whatever."

He put them all back and hid them in the same spot again. "Do you hate us?"

I wasn't sure how to respond. "Why would you ask me that?"

"You never came to see us." His eyes blinked slowly, like he was waiting for me to come up with an explanation.

For a while, even before Terese had aroused my suspicions that day in the gym, I sometimes wondered if the staleness of our existence would slowly suffocate us. I finally understood why Mom and Terese and Lexie doted on the Supplements. Sitting with Lucas, my brother, I already felt different. More alive than I'd felt for a long time.

I explained it to him. "It was dumb of me to stay away. Let's just leave it at that."

He nodded. "I have to get my pie-jammas on now." He skipped off to where Terese was helping a little girl with dark braids put on a nightgown.

In the rocking chair, Lexie held the youngest one, a boy about a year old. I heard her call him Quinn. I'd always considered my older sister to be completely self-absorbed, concerned only with herself and what she could gain from any situation. Her actions usually proved my assumptions to be true. But as I observed her, she was unaware of being watched.

Lexie held Quinn with a look on her face I'd never seen. If I had to describe it, I guess I could say she appeared happy. Not because she was getting her way or someone was doing something for her. She was just content in the role of observing Quinn, just waiting to see what he would do next. Mostly I was amazed to see her being so patient with someone.

Then Lexie saw me. "What are you doing down here?" Before I could answer, her surprised look turned to one of annoyance and she stood up, shoving Quinn into my arms. "Hold him, I have to pee."

I tried to hand him back. "Wait, don't leave."

She was already into the bathroom on the other side of the suite. Terese had her hands full. I was stuck. I wanted to let go, drop him, anything to get him out of my arms. But he was clutching me so hard. So I held Quinn.

My hands on his waist, I tried to lean as far away as I

could. He struggled to twist around and face me, patting my face with his hands. Blond hair curled around his ears. His footed pajamas were made of soft polar fleece, a blue and white print with moose and pine trees. His heavy, solid toddler body radiated heat. He smelled of baby shampoo and powder, not unpleasant in the least.

I shifted him up a bit to get a better grip.

He giggled, revealing two tiny front teeth.

"Do you like him?" Lucas padded over dressed in similar pajamas. "That's Quinn."

"Yeah, I know."

"So do you like him?"

Quinn patted my face and inspected my nose. I cringed, but still squeaked out a reply. "He's cute." He was.

Lexie came back out and took Quinn. "Thanks. Wasn't that bad, was it?" Lexie set Quinn inside a playpen.

My hands trembled as I wiped my sweaty face on my shirt. I wished my heart would stop pounding so hard.

Lucas pulled on my shirt. "We can do Legos now."

"Yeah, okay. You go get ready and I'll be right there." I waited until he couldn't hear me, then I said to Lexie, "We need to talk."

On the other side of the room, Lucas dumped all the Legos on the floor.

Quinn squawked.

Lexie reached down and hoisted Quinn out of the playpen. He grabbed a fistful of her hair. She winced, holding his hand so he couldn't yank any more. Lexie hid her face in Quinn's chest as he squealed.

"Lex, you don't have to go along with any of Dad's plans."

Her reply was muffled. "And see how long it takes us to starve?"

"I just had a talk with Dad. He showed me the lab."

She didn't say anything.

"He said he'd talked to you."

She nodded.

"It's true? Have you been to the lab? Seen what he plans to do?"

Lexie fixed her dark eyes on me. "If it was the only way, I would do it."

I tried to make my voice sound as kind as possible, not exactly a practiced skill of mine. "Lex, even if there were more, you would come to love them, just like you love these ones."

She chewed on the inside of her cheek, then set Quinn on the ground where he crawled off toward Terese. "Meet me later. In my room, after Terese has gone to bed."

"Why?"

"I need to know what you know. I have to decide what to do. Eli, we're wasting time." She laughed without sounding the least bit cheerful. "How stupid is that? We have all the time in the world, years and years. Yet it's all so urgent."

"Eli!" Lucas sat amid a mountain of Legos, waving. "I'm ready."

Lexie left before I could catch her, so I stayed with Lucas. We built a tower halfway. I wanted something bigger.

Digging in the closet, I lifted a container from the top shelf and discovered a shrink-wrapped, unopened box of Legos, along with other unused, brand-new toys.

Another one of Dad's stashes. I found a bag of balloons and told Lucas I'd be right out. I blew up a few, red and purple and green. I opened the door and freed them. They floated out toward the others and bounced along the ground.

Lucas clapped. "Yay!"

The little girl stopped playing and stared.

Terese called out, "Go get it, Cara!"

Cara kicked one, traipsing after to kick it again.

Terese held Quinn as she picked up a balloon. She held it out to him.

He grinned. "Bub-oh."

I didn't understand. "What did he say?"

Terese giggled. "Bubble. He thinks it's a bubble, like in the bubble bath."

Bubble baths? Of course. Of course the children had bubble baths. Of course they had that part of childhood. What else had I missed all that time?

Terese enunciated her words. "It's a balloon, Quinn. Balloon."

"Boon?"

Terese nodded. "Yes, balloon."

"Boon. My boon."

My face flushed. My upper lip broke out in sweat. I excused myself.

In the hallway I squatted, leaning my head against the

wall. As much as I'd tried to remain detached, unaffected, I'd been touched. Touched and affected. Because no matter what I might call them, no matter what the unholy reason for their creation, the simple fact remained: the Supplements were a part of me.

They were part of all of us.

As I sat there considering the Supplements and their intended purpose, Dad's other repugnant solution for the food shortage, it made me wonder. Had we become godless?

Were we so removed from the world of before that we would actually consider such things to be commonplace?

Mundane?

Another fact of life?

God forbid: not immoral?

I'd been a practicing selfish worm for so long. Basically my entire life. Why was I suddenly so opposed to doing the very things that would ensure my continued existence? Given the context, the circumstances that no one had ever faced before, there really wasn't a precedent. We were it. Was it the right thing then? To do what was necessary, no matter what?

I had never made a point of seeking out right and wrong. The right answer depended entirely on whether the outcome benefited me. Right or wrong, this outcome would definitely benefit me, more than any other outcome had before.

This time, however, I felt it. I felt it in my head. I felt it in my heart. Dad's solutions were wrong. And for once, I was not going to do the wrong thing.

We had not become godless. The Compound had just distracted us. We still needed to live by rules of the old world, even if those rules didn't exist anymore. They were a line that could not be crossed. For the first time that I could remember, I was going to take a stand.

I wasn't Eddy. Didn't pretend to be.

But I could still, for once in my life, do the right thing.

CHAPTER THIRTEEN

LATER, I SHOWED UP AT LEXIE'S DOOR IN A T-SHIRT AND jeans. I was barefoot. My hair was down and I tucked it behind my ears.

Lexie opened the door, wearing a white terry robe.

·I had one just like it. We all did.

Her hair was damp and loose, looking like she'd showered recently. She seemed a bit unsteady. She ushered me inside, not saying anything. Janis Joplin was loud on the stereo.

I hadn't been in her room since the first night in the Compound, when Dad had taken us on the tour. There had never been a reason for me to go in there and she certainly never had a reason to invite me. The room looked different. The Arabian Nights theme had been replaced by abstract murals with earthy tones. They were skilled renderings that impressed me.

"Did you paint these?"

She rolled her eyes. "No, we hired outside help."

I studied the artwork more. She must have spent a lot of time on it. Strange to think such a change had occurred without my knowing about it.

But then, the walls of my cocoon were thick.

She sat down on her bed. The cover was a simple white crocheted bedspread over a pink satin comforter. Dozens of pillows in various colors, no doubt carryovers from the harem motif, covered the headboard. Lexie crossed her legs and stretched her robe down to cover them.

"Dad told me . . . about his solution to the food problem."

Her eyes narrowed. "I'll do it, you know. If that's what it takes. I already decided."

I took a step toward her. "You can't!"

She crossed her arms and leaned back. "You don't get a say."

I sat down on the edge of her bed. "Please. Just listen to me."

Her chin tilted down and she looked sideways at me. She shrugged. "Fine. Talk."

"Lex, everything about it is wrong. Cloning a human is . . . frickin' twisted. In so many ways. It's like playing God, creating another life like that." I shook my head. "And the reasoning behind it, that's even worse."

"Want to hear my reasons?"

I did. "Yeah."

She held up one finger at a time as she said the names of the three children in the yellow room.

"I don't understand."

She sighed. "Don't you see? If I start producing clones, I can save them. Lucas and Cara and Quinn. We won't have to . . . *use* them."

I shook my head. "How do you figure that?"

She shrugged. "Well, don't clones grow faster than the real thing? So they would get bigger faster and . . ."

My words were a shout. "There haven't been any human clones before! No one knows what will happen. Maybe it won't even work."

Her words were a whisper. "I have to try."

I leaned forward, staring at my feet. My hair fell around my face so that I was inside of a tent. A shelter of my own making where I could hide. But not really. "This is so messed up."

Something rattled. "Tic Tac?"

I sat back up and laughed. Because at that point, it was laugh or cry.

"What's so funny?" Lexie poured some into her hand and tossed the container to me.

I caught it as I pushed my hair back. "That's what was in your special treat box. Tic Tacs." I picked up the container and shook several directly into my mouth. The refreshing minty taste was a holiday for my sheltered taste buds.

She waited.

Was she expecting something from me? "I'm not letting you go through with this."

"Dad will make me, anyway, so it's no use even——"

"Dad can't make you."

She chewed on her lip. "Hello. He can make us do whatever he wants. He's in control here."

I was a little taken aback by how resigned she was, like she had no choice. "I thought you said Mom was."

Her eyes got teary. "He told me that Mom knows what he wants us to do. That's why she's not talking to him. And she knows she can't stop him."

It dawned on me. So that's why Mom didn't want Dad to know about the flour. She knew he was already considering extreme measures involving Lexie. The flour situation alone would have driven him to his decision. The results of the inventory did it instead. "I can stop him."

She wiped her eyes with the back of her hand. "How?"

"Remember your little speech? You were right, I do have to choose. And I choose not to be on his side."

She shook her head. "What if we do run out of food? And this was our chance to save ourselves and we wouldn't do it and . . ."

"Lexie, he's been lying to us, lying to us about so many things. I think I believe the world is not as he says. That it's not that bad outside."

"*I think I believe?*" She rolled her eyes. "That's supposed to mean something when we're starving or dying from radiation sickness if we do get outside?"

I hid my face in my hands and groaned. "I know. I know it sounds crazy." My hands slid down, uncovering my eyes. "It means you have to trust me. You have to be on my side."

Her head dipped to one side. "I don't know, Eli. At least Dad has a plan."

My hands slammed into the bed on either side of me. "I do, too!"

"What is it?" She crossed her arms.

Could I trust her? Trust that she wouldn't go running to Dad? "I think . . . I think I can get connected to the Internet."

Lexie gaped at me. Her mouth fell open slightly.

I nodded. "Dad told me it's up, just a bit spotty. He won't let me on it. I think he's hiding something. If I can just get to his office when he has it powered up, I can find out."

Her hands flew out, palms up. "Find out what?"

"I don't know, just talk to someone. See what their situation is. If they've heard about the rest of the world . . ." I trailed off.

It all sounded pretty lame, even to me.

Lexie leaned back. There was an odd expression on her face. "One day."

What did she mean by that? I held up my hands. "What?"

"I'll give you one day, twenty-four hours, to find out what you can. And if this is just one of your stupid stunts to get what you want, you will be so sorry. I swear." She frowned. "You can leave now."

I headed to my room to figure out a plan. Just past the Supplements' room, I narrowly avoided a collision with Dad.

"Eli, you okay?"

I willed my heart to slow down. For some reason, I was afraid he could read my thoughts. I lied. "I . . . I spent some time with the Supplements."

Dad smirked. "That Lucas is a kick, huh? Smart kid. I daresay, smarter than you even were at that age." He scratched his head.

My head cocked to the side. "You spend time with them?"

Dad made a strange face. "What, I'm not supposed to go near them? That's a little unrealistic, don't you think? Who do you think watches them while the rest of you have music?"

My mouth dropped open. I didn't understand how he could be with them, take care of them, yet still . . . "But how—"

He blew it off with a toss of one hand, as if it were nothing; a mere gnat on an elephant's ass. "When the time comes, we'll do what's necessary. Until then, I wouldn't go to the nursery too often. It'll make it all the harder for you."

That conversation confirmed one thing: I really didn't know my father at all. I watched him walk toward his office. Then I chided myself for just standing there. It was the perfect opportunity to try the Internet again. The laptop was under my bed. I also grabbed a legal pad and a pen and took a few seconds to put my hair in a sloppy ponytail.

First I peeked around the corner. The office door was closed. Music was playing. Sounded like Neil Young. At least it was loud, which made this as good a time as any. I sat in the same place as before and switched on the laptop, making sure the sound was muted.

My breaths were shallow.

Come on. Come on.

There it was.

Wireless Network Now Connected.

Holy crap.

For a few moments, I sat there, not believing. The world was once again at my fingertips. What did I do first?

My hands trembled. Partly from the words on the screen and the power they conveyed. Partly from Dad being so close. Before I could make my first move, my instant messaging icon popped up.

Welcome TwinYan2! The following buddies are online:

With a shaking hand, I scrolled down.

TwinYan1

Eddy?

CHAPTER FOURTEEN

Eddy? How could that be?

I didn't stop to think. I just typed. **Eddy? RUT?** *Dummy. There's no way.* Still, I held my breath.

A reply popped up. **WTHIT?**

Who the hell is this? My breath gushed out. Great. Some irate survivor. What could they do to me? Take away my birthday? I typed again. **Eli.**

Again, an instant reply. **how did u get his username? lose it before I find out WTH U R.**

My heart sped up. **eddy! it's eli. swear.**

Nothing.

I added more. **we're in compound. near cabin.** I didn't have to wait long.

how u know about that?

The tremor in my hands made it difficult to type as fast as I wanted. **camping. had fight about who in Dad's plane**

1st? kitten in **RV. wheezing** . . . I didn't want to write what happened next. I skipped to **we had to go.**

A few minutes passed.

AYTMTB?

I groaned. **cuz true!**

you read it in paper.

What was he talking about? I scrolled back up, to see the whole conversation. Crap. I'd provided all the details. I could be IM'ing anybody. My stomach clenched—it could even be Dad. Or could it? One way to find out.

what was in red cooler at picnic with gram?

The screen stayed blank. Then: **eli?**

I wasn't falling for it. **what was in cooler?**

strawberry mochi

One of my hands went over my mouth. No one could have known that except Eddy or Gram. My fingers flew. **OMG. Eddy????**

His answer came fast. **AAS**

Alive and smiling. My eyes teared up.

Where ru? ru alone?

What was he talking about? **we're in compound. we escaped attack.**

what attack?

What did he mean by that? Again, I wondered if it was really Eddy, or if it was just someone screwing with me. **nukes. dad knew. got us in compound, but u & gram didn't make it back.** As I typed, I thought of more questions. **how did u survive? where ru?**

The reply took a few minutes. **eli, don't know what u r**

talking about. gram & i home. seattle. we saw fire from cabin. fire dept came—it all gone.

Inside the office, inches away from me, Dad's chair creaked.

I froze.

The music still blared.

My hands started up again, trembling. **what gone?**

RV. cops said RV crashed into plane, burned. At funeral, nothing to bury.

Fire? Funeral?

Both of my hands clamped over my mouth.

I rocked back and forth, forcing a scream back down.

No, it wasn't true. That wasn't what happened.

eli RUT?

My breaths became gasps as I typed; trying to prove it wasn't true. **not dead! here in compound! ALIVE! dad stopped RV, we ran here.**

where compound?

IDK! where we camped, but then drove & ran.

There wasn't a reply right away. I prayed I wasn't making too much noise, that my dad wouldn't come out. *Come on, come on.*

Eli, this is Gram. Are you all ok? Clea and your sisters? Tell me where you are.

Gram. My gram. My eyes misted over. **all fine in compound.**

We thought you all died in the fire.

No, no, no! It's a lie. **dad said you and E died. we have to stay 15 years and**

I couldn't say any more. It was too hard. I hit the Send button.

Gram had her own form of IM speak. **Lying SOB. We will get you out.**

I didn't know what to say in reply, so I didn't type anything.

E here. gram freaking, yelling at els to call 911. thought compound just myth. tabloids right about dad—major nutcase.

What tabloids?

?????

after we thought you dead, report from secret source. dad's biological mom crazy.

It made so much sense. All those times when he wouldn't sleep for days. And then the times that's all he did. All the talking to himself. Only he wasn't, not to *him*. *He* heard someone talking back.

get you out, bro, swear.

I held my head in my hands, thinking. It was true, everything. My father lied, kept us down here with the lies. That night when his hands smelled like fuel and he was so out of breath. He'd been setting the RV on fire.

The low-battery warning flashed. I ignored it.

The facts started to sink in.

I wanted to run to my father.

Make him let us out.

Then I realized something. Dad wouldn't let us out. We were prisoners.

u have to find us.

Eddy's reply was short but meant everything to me.

BTWBO.

Be there with bells on.

The low-battery warning flashed again. "No!"

Dad's chair squeaked and the music went dead.

I slammed the laptop shut.

My stomach clenched again.

I didn't want to lose the connection with Eddy. I didn't want to be alone again. I tried to reassure myself. Now that we'd been in touch once, we could do it again. I would find out everything I could, anything that might help Eddy find us. If we worked together, we could do it.

He had saved me before. He could do it again.

The door opened. Dad scanned the hallway. "Eli, need help?" He must have seen the confused look on my face.

"Oh, uh, yeah. Just some math again. I think I just figured it out." I held up the legal pad.

He stood there, clenching and unclenching his hands.

"What's wrong?"

"Nothing. Feels like pins and needles. Must be too much typing. What's this?" Before I could stop him, he lifted the computer from my lap.

"No." I grabbed on to it.

He didn't let go.

We stood there, both gripping the laptop, a mostly mental tug of war.

His head tilted a bit. "Where did you get this?"

"Eddy's room." As soon as I said it, I knew I should have lied.

But from the look on his face, I think he already sensed the answer. I think he was mad at himself for forgetting it was there.

I held my breath and shut my eyes. The IM conversation was still on the screen for him to see.

I heard the click as it shut down. My eyes opened. The battery was dead. I breathed out.

Dad shrugged. "This one is nearly obsolete. It doesn't have the functions you need. I'll take care of it for you."

I couldn't risk raising his suspicions any more before I found out what I needed to know. My hands let go. I was only able to watch as my connection to Eddy disappeared with Dad into his office.

He came back out and handed me another laptop, a different model. Then he retreated once again.

I didn't even have to look at the laptop to know there would be no connection to the Internet.

I hugged my knees. My head dropped onto them and my eyes closed. It was all true. My own father kept us here, prisoners. Without that laptop, I wouldn't be able to tell Eddy anything to help him find us.

There were two things of which I was certain.

First, I was on my own.

Second, my own father had become the enemy.

Maybe he always had been. Furious, I wanted to barge into his office and demand he let us out. I wanted to scream at him, hit him. I jumped up, my hands turned into fists as I faced his door. My breath was shallow and fast as I stood there, ready to fight for all of us, make him let us out.

It took every ounce of self-control in me to walk the other way, go to my room, and shut the door. I couldn't let him know what I knew. Not yet.

I needed to get back in touch with Eddy. There hadn't been enough time to tell him what I knew. I thought about it. What *did* I know that could help him find us?

Nothing.

I had no clue where the hatch was. Dad had mentioned there were GPS coordinates. And a code. Knowing him, they were only in his brain. He never liked a paper trail. No way would he tell me what I needed to know. Not straight out. I would have to find out on my own.

The world was fine. Dad knew. He knew that it had gone on without us. That it *was* going on without us every minute we stayed down here. He had to be insane. Nothing else made sense.

My dread mingled with hope—Eddy and Gram were alive! I wanted to run, tell everyone. But I knew there was only one person I could trust.

The door to Lexie's room was slightly ajar. The TV was on.

I pushed the door open a little more so I could see in. At first I didn't see her. She was leaning on the footboard of her bed, arms around her knees. She stared at the screen.

I figured it was her horror movie routine.

But her face was shiny. Was she crying? No way.

The DVD player was on, and I recognized the movie. *A Little Princess.* One of the premieres we went to in

Hollywood. Not my favorite. But I knew it was based on a classic book and it had a happy ending.

Over the sound of the movie, I heard Lexie take a loud, ragged breath.

Just like she did with the horror movies, she stared at the screen, engrossed. But for this movie, her eyes weren't blank. They were full, full of so many feelings I couldn't start to name them all.

It didn't seem right, to be a witness. I felt invasive, like an intruder.

Back in the hall, I gently pulled the door shut and left.

Maybe that was when Lexie let it all out. She watched *A Little Princess*, the one happy ending she allowed herself.

Who else was there for me to turn to?

I couldn't tell Mom. Not yet. She was already stressed out, pregnant. And I wasn't sure she'd believe me. Even if she did, it was way too risky for her to confront my father. She was in no condition for it. And did she even have a foothold with him anymore?

Maybe if I had found this out years ago. When they were in love. When he still doted on her. Not at this point. They scarcely spoke.

I didn't understand how he could do this to us, the people he was supposed to love the most. When did he start hating us? Because he must have hated us, if he could even consider doing this. It was the only explanation I had that made sense.

There was a slim chance he had confided in Mom at some point, told her something that might help.

I felt so stupid for waiting so long to question things.
For being this much of a sheep.
Listening to everything Dad said.
Believing him.
Worshipping him.
No more. No way.
I was done.

CHAPTER FIFTEEN

Sleep eluded me. I spent most of the night staring up into the starry sky of my ceiling, trying to come up with answers. But in all that sleeplessness I made a decision. A decision to seek the answers I needed.

The next morning, I found Mom in the family room, knitting another pink and blue blanket. Candles glowed. The scent of flowers lingered. Music played on the stereo, a sonata for cello and piano—Shostokavich.

I sat down on a couch opposite her. The soft, familiar brush of my hair falling on either side of my face gave me strength, but it still took a minute to get the words out. "Mom, do you know the code to the door?"

Her knitting needles froze as she stared at me. "How do you know about that?"

"Dad told me."

Her hands dropped to her lap, the ball of pink yarn

unrolling onto the floor. She seemed annoyed. "Now why in the world would he tell you that?"

I explained. And then I asked again. "Do you know the code to the door?"

She harrumphed. (I think that's what the sound would be called. Like a sarcastic cough.) "Right. That's only in your father's mind. And probably in his office."

"Do you know where?"

She started knitting again, her stitches quick and precise. "Probably in one of his computers."

I leaned my head back on the couch, trying to think. "Mom, what if something happens to him? How would we get out?"

She set down her knitting. "Don't talk like that. Nothing's going to happen to your father, Eli. He's as healthy as a horse." Her tone was not one of certainty and her words were rushed.

"Mom?"

She shook her head a bit. "He's healthier than a horse, probably. And if he thought he was going to die, God forbid, he'd tell me everything."

Somehow I doubted it. "Would he?"

Her brow furrowed. "What's going on?"

My eyes shut briefly. I rubbed my temples, trying to summon more energy. "Mom, I found something out last night. Something you might not believe."

"Tell me."

My explanation included everything about the laptop

from Eddy's room and its wireless capability. I paused for a moment before getting to the crucial element.

"Mom, I talked to Eddy."

Her knitting slid to the floor. "You *what*?"

"The Internet works. I IM'ed Eddy. And Gram. Dad's been lying to us since we got here." I related everything Eddy and Gram had to say.

Mom just sat there, mouth gaping.

I needed her to trust me. "Please say you believe me."

Her face crumpled. I knew for certain, then and there, that she truly had no idea what Dad had done. She started to cry.

"Please, Mom."

She nodded, reaching out for my hand.

I didn't move.

Her hand dropped in her lap. When she could speak again, she had a lot of questions.

I answered the ones I could. There were many that I couldn't.

"Eli, we have got to go to your father and tell him it's over. We know and we're leaving."

I stood up and started to pace in front of the fireplace. "Do you think it's that easy? He'll just throw up his hands and say, 'You got me,' and then let us go?"

Her head was down. "No. It won't be that easy."

"He's insane."

"Eli, he's not insane."

I protested, telling her what Eddy had said about Dad's biological mother.

Mom shook her head. "It's not true. That's an old rumor, one I even approached your father about before you were born. He found out who his biological parents were a long time ago."

"And?"

"A couple of academically inclined teenagers too stupid to use birth control. And too young and full of potential to give it all up to raise a baby. No one was crazy."

I was frustrated at not getting my point across. "Mom. Look at the facts. Dad doesn't sleep for days, then that's all he does."

Mom shrugged. "I don't think that's an uncommon thing with creative geniuses. And it's not enough to make him certifiable."

I groaned and covered my face with my hands.

"Eli. I would love to say yes, that he's insane. But that's simply too easy. And safe. How convenient would that be? To explain it away to lunacy?" Her head tilted to one side. "He was lucid when he planned all this. He's still lucid. That's what scares me."

I dropped my hands to look at her.

She turned toward me, her face red and tear streaked. "Yes, I'm scared. I said it. We're in more danger now than we ever have been, Eli. If he knows we know, he may get desperate. I don't believe he's crazy, but he's capable of do-ing something . . . something irrational."

I held my arms out to the sides. "More irrational than all of this? More irrational than every moment of the last six years?"

Her expression wasn't quite a smile. "You have a point, my boy." She gasped. "Oh!"

"You okay?"

Her hands went to her bump. "The baby's kicking all the time. Whatever we're going to do, we need to do it fast. I refuse to have another of my children born in this godforsaken place. We need to see what we can find out without your father suspecting we're fishing around. So let's keep it between us. I don't think you should tell Lexie or Terese."

"Tell me what?" Lexie stepped inside the room. She looked fresh in yellow, her dark hair cascading loose.

"Nothing, sweetie."

"Right." Lexie sunk into the love seat opposite of us. "I heard you say, 'Don't tell Lexie or Terese.'"

I leaned against the mantel. I should have told her what I knew last night. "Now is not the time for this, okay? Just trust me. It doesn't matter anymore."

Lexie crossed her arms, glaring at Mom. "I know there are a billion things you're keeping from me. Tell me."

"Lex—"

"Eli!" She nearly snarled at me. "Stay out of it. Mom, tell me. Tell me what you don't want me to know."

"Sweetie, it's about the code."

"What code?"

"For the door. We were talking about the code and that only your father knows what it is."

Lexie rolled her eyes. "What's the big secret?"

Mom held out a hand to Lexie. "We didn't want you to worry about it. Please don't tell Terese, okay?"

narrowed. "I don't believe you."

. . . throat. "Lex, it's true. No one else knows."

. . . , I get that. I think you were talking about some-
. . . g else."

Mom picked up her knitting again, the red metal needles clicking in her hands.

Lexie glared at her. "Look at me." Lexie leaned forward, her face flushed. Her voice was deep, harsh. "I hate
that you just tell me something and I'm supposed to take it.
I hate that you're the queen and we have to do everything
you say. All you did was marry a rich guy and have his
kids. That's it, that's all you are."

Any sympathy I may have felt for her the night before
evaporated. "Shut up!" I screamed.

Mom looked at Lexie. "I know you don't mean that."

Lex turned her glare to me. "You're her lapdog, you do
whatever she says."

I retaliated by calling her a name, and I didn't bother to
use Mandarin.

"Eli, don't talk to your sister like that."

Dad entered the room, his glance bouncing between the
three of us. "What's all the yelling? I could hear you down
the hall."

Lexie pouted. "They won't tell me what they're talking
about." She looked from one parent to the other. "You both
treat me like a child."

Mom fidgeted with her knitting.

Dad scratched his chin. "Lexie, your mother and I know
what's best for you, for all of you."

With all that I knew, it was impossible to just stand there and say nothing. "You mean you *think* you know best."

"I do know best." Before he said it, Dad had hesitated.

Barely, but I saw it. Which gave me the strength to say what I needed to. "I don't think only you knowing the code for the door is the best thing, Dad."

"And who else should know? You?" He laughed.

My hands clenched.

"Eli, you are young and impulsive. One bad day and you'd be wanting out."

If he only knew. I went for it. "Why do you get to be the one to make all the decisions?"

Dad's expression changed. Became hard. "Why? Because I built this place, it's mine. I *should* make all the decisions."

I couldn't stop. "And the rest of us? You own us, too?"

Dad shook his head. He set a hand on his stomach, wincing. "That's not what I meant."

"Bull!" This wasn't how I planned it. Too late. My emotions were running the show. "I got on the Internet, I talked to Eddy. You've lied to us from the beginning— there was no nuclear attack—it was all a lie. We could have left here any time. Any frickin' time!" My tone was a screech by the time I got done.

Mom didn't even tell me to watch my language as her eyes squeezed shut and she gripped her knitting needles so hard that her knuckles turned white.

Lexie stood up. Her forehead wrinkled as she processed what I'd said. She sank into the couch next to

Mom, apparently forgetting her animosity of moments before.

I suddenly wished I had told Lexie about Eddy and the Internet before. She deserved to know. But I wasn't done. "When I think of everything you made us *believe*. The things you would have made us *do*." I looked at Lexie before turning back to Dad. "And none of them were necessary. Not even one. This place wasn't our sanctuary. This was *your* world. Your twisted world."

Dad looked from Mom to Lexie, then back to me. His face held no expression. "I wanted to save my family from the largest menace of the modern age. I'm *twisted* for wanting to save my family?"

"But there was no nuclear attack to save us from!"

His voice was calm. "You don't know that. You have no way of knowing what the truth is and what isn't."

How could he say that?

"I do! I talked to Eddy and Gram and they told me everything. . . ." I trailed off, sounding like a little kid trying to talk his way out of getting grounded for something inane like shaving the family cat.

Dad scratched his head. "I'm not sure what kind of person you've become, if you fault me that much for ensuring the survival of my wife and children."

"I know what happened!" My voice quavered, which only served to make me more determined. I was not going to back down. "You did this to us, you set it all up. There were no nukes. I know it. I can't prove it, but I know it's the truth. And now you have to give me the code, so we can get out."

My hair had fallen in front of my eyes and I slowly pushed it back. I forced myself to calm down, sound rational for my last plea. "Just let us go, Dad. After all this time, you owe us that."

His eyebrows lowered and his voice was thunder. "I am your father. I owe you nothing."

"Oh my God." Mom stood up, her face red, her hands trembling. "Is it true?"

Dad didn't look at her.

Mom dropped back down on the couch beside Lexie, who was crying. "Is it, Rex? Was this all a joke to you?"

He met her eyes. "No, Clea. Not a joke. It was never that."

"What about me?" Mom shook her head in disbelief. "You told me my son and my mother were dead and I believed you. My God, all these years I trusted you."

Their eyes locked. She was the first to look away. Dad gazed at her a moment more, then crossed his arms, his shoulders slumped. "No one is leaving. You can't. Okay, so Eli thinks he had a chat with someone. That doesn't change a thing. The door isn't opening until the time is up. We've got nine years left. It's my plan and I'm not changing it."

Mom put her hands over her face and spoke through them. "Why would you leave Eddy out?"

"I didn't plan to." Dad's voice was softer than before. He stepped backward until he bumped into a bar stool and climbed onto it, gripping the edge of the bar for balance. "I just wanted to leave your mother out. So I left the kitten for Terese to find, I knew she'd bring it along. And I knew your mother would run back to the cabin for Eddy's medicine. That was key, I think." He shrugged. "To leave part of the family out there to mourn us. It made it all the more believable and tragic. However, I didn't plan on Eddy going with her." He held a hand out toward my mom. "Please believe me, Clea. That hurt me as much as it did you. But it was too late by then."

Mom dropped her hands and walked over to him. "But *I* didn't know!" Her face was so red and her eyes were nearly slits. I had never seen her that angry. "You told me my son and my mother were dead and I believed you. All these years I believed you." Tears spilled onto her cheeks. She stepped forward and slapped him. Hard.

Dad put a hand up to his cheek. His voice was almost pleading. "Believe me, that broke my heart. Seeing your pain. But the deception was necessary for my plan."

I wanted to kill him. "Some plan. You screwed up, Dad. The feed, the bulbs."

His voice was a whisper. "Those weren't entirely an accident."

Mom stepped back and grabbed Lexie's hand.

I couldn't speak.

"I wanted to create the need for an alternate food source. I'd mentioned it to my . . . my planners, but I didn't know for sure how they would make it happen. At the time the livestock died, I was so frustrated. Nothing had been going as I'd planned and I wondered if I should give up. But then I realized it was the perfect opportunity." His cheek was an angry red. "Those issues created the perfect need for an alternate food source. What I came to call the Donner Effect."

Lexie was incredulous. "Like those pioneer people who all ate each other? You would have let us die?"

Dad's expression softened. "No, of course not. Don't you think the world thought the people on the Oregon Trail were crazy? To leave solid, contented lives for some stupid quest? They weren't crazy, they were brave. Brave and determined. Our life we were living, our oh-so-easy life, didn't give any of you a chance to be brave or determined."

He stopped to scratch his neck. "No, you would have grown up not knowing what it's like to have to work, to strive. I wanted to see if we could do it, if our family would really have what it takes to survive." He paused for a moment. "I have enough money to do anything, go anywhere. To take my children anywhere, buy them anything they want. How long would that have kept us satisfied? Before I even married your mother, I had already discovered that about money. Eventually you run out of things to buy. No, that's not quite it." He seemed to search for the right words. "Eventually you run out of things to buy that truly make you happy."

Lexie broke in, speaking between sobs. "You had all of us. Didn't we make you happy?"

Dad pulled a roll of antacid tablets out of his pocket. They were crumbly, in small pieces, so he sprinkled the remnants into his hand. He raised his hand to his mouth, then chewed before continuing. "Yes, Lexie. Of course. You all mean more to me than anything. I wanted to show you the world. But what would be left once you had seen everything, done everything?"

He leaned an elbow on the bar. "I didn't want you to feel like I did, that the world had a limit on new experiences. I didn't want you to feel like all the pioneering is over. The world out there doesn't provide challenges like this. No one has ever done this before. I wanted us to be pioneers. I wanted to prove that we can do it. We will be the only people to theoretically survive a nuclear winter."

"That's it?" I shrugged when I would rather have screamed. "Couldn't we have just hopped a flight to the moon?"

"Any idiot with a million dollars will be able to do that soon." Dad chuckled a little. "Oh, come on, there's always a bottom line. Even as we speak I'm working on a more conventional, readily available prototype of the Compound. Because once we emerge and share our story, everyone will want one of these for themselves." He spread his arms out wide for emphasis, then dropped them to his side. "For their families. So they can survive. And they will thank us for proving it can be done as they follow in our footsteps. Just like the people who followed those first pioneers into the West."

I groaned. "And what, the Supplements were just meant to be collateral damage?"

Dad shook his head. "I never would have touched them,

not in that way. They're our children"—he nodded at Mom—"as much as any of you are."

Lexie stood up. "How can you say that?" She flung one arm in the direction of the hallway. "They've been stuck in that yellow room since they were born."

"And what's so bad about the yellow room? What did you have as a child that they don't?"

"Everything!" Lexie cried. "A real school. Friends."

"Friends?" Dad rolled his eyes. "None of you kids ever had a friend that wasn't there for your money or your last name."

Mom wiped her eyes as she spoke up. "There's something to be said for fresh air and sunshine."

Dad nodded. "Yes. But they've also never seen violence on TV or been snowed over by advertisements. They don't sit in front of the television and beg for everything they see. They aren't brats like—"

Oh God. Like me. They weren't brats like me.

Lexie gasped. "Like us? Is that what you were going to say?"

Dad turned to me. "Do you know when this Compound turned for me?"

I didn't understand.

"I began building this place solely for survival. When you boys were born. I truly hoped we would never have to enter it as a family. In the beginning, that's all it was. A safety net. Do you want to know when it turned into something else?"

I wasn't sure if I did or not. "Yes."

"You were seven. We went to the Rockies after Christmas."

My breath caught in my throat, remembering. Our house in Colorado was part of the Rockies Club, a spectacular gated community with its own private ski hill. Our house was the biggest and most elaborate, the only one with a heated mile-long driveway, so that it would always stay clear for Dad to get to the helicopter pad in case he needed to leave for business.

"Remember, Eli?"

I nodded.

"I got a call from D.C. during a heavy snowfall. I planned to fly out the next morning after the snow stopped."

I didn't want to remember.

I went outside after dark to the propane tank, the forty-thousand-gallon tank that heated the driveway. So Dad could go wherever he needed to. So he could leave us again, screw up another family vacation for work. Screw up my plans for the next day. I wanted him to stay, wanted him to watch me on my new snowboard, wanted him to make hot chocolate afterward. So I turned off the valve on the tank. It was easy, the caretaker had shown me one day so I would quit bothering him. And in the morning—

"I couldn't get out of the driveway. Remember, Eli? And you confessed. You cried, said you only wanted me to stay. You wanted me to be with you all the time, every day."

I covered my eyes with one hand.

"I realized I was screwing up, leaving you all so much

for work. And I didn't want to anymore. I wanted to be with you all the time. Like you wanted me to be with you, son."

And once again, I had gotten what I wanted.

I dropped my hand and looked at my father. No way was I taking the blame. "That doesn't explain the rest of it. The food . . . the babies . . . God, the cloning?" I looked at Lexie.

Lexie looked back at me, her face shiny with tears.

He sighed. "That was merely a matter of seeing how far you would all go to survive."

Mom let out a cry. She launched herself toward Dad, pummeling him with her fists.

He shoved her away, not unkindly.

Still, I lost it.

With every ounce of my strength and rage, I punched him in the face.

I'd never hit anyone before. The feel of his bones and flesh connecting with my hand sickened me. And it hurt. But touching him didn't bother me. Or stop me from hitting him again. With my extra five inches of height and a good thirty pounds on him, it was no contest.

Lexie jumped onto my back, trying to stop me as blood spurted from his nose. Her arms were tight around my neck, her breathing heavy and warm in my ear, her body a dead weight on my back.

I paused at the sensation, wanting to freak out. To run away. But it wasn't enough to stop me.

Dad lost his balance and fell off the stool. It looked like

he was in slow motion. His head bounced on the floor. He slammed to a stop into the oak bar, and then was still.

With Lexie on my back, I straddled him. His neck was hot under my hands as I watched him through my veil of hair and gripped tighter, wanting to choke the life from him.

Lexie's arms grew tighter around my neck until I couldn't breathe. She pulled me back, away from him as she screamed. "Stop it! Stop it!"

Sweat dripped down my back.

My heart raced.

I'd been touched and I had touched and I was still alive. Only thing was, I didn't know if Dad still was.

CHAPTER SIXTEEN

My knuckles were covered in blood. I didn't know if it was mine or his.

I backed away and Lexie finally got off. I felt so light without her.

Mom knelt by Dad. "Rex?"

He groaned. His eyes stayed closed. He didn't utter any other sounds.

"Mom?" Lexie's voice was shaky. She turned to me, her face red and blotched. "What did you do? Now we'll never get out!"

Had I just messed up everything? I let my hair stay where it was, covering my face.

Mom's voice was strong. "Eli, go get a gurney. We need to get him to the infirmary."

My legs wouldn't move.

Mom spoke again, firm but quiet. "Eli, go."

I stumbled from the room, my breaths shallow and

rapid. I staggered from one side of the hallway to the other, my hair obscuring my view, and I held a hand to my chest as I ran. My heart felt like it was going to explode. When I reached the infirmary, I bent over for a moment and caught my breath. As fast as I could, I pushed a gurney back to them. I'd picked one with squeaky wheels, and they were the only sound besides our breathing as we rolled Dad to the infirmary and got him into a bed.

Mom's face was red and tear stained, and she struggled to catch her breath as she sat beside Dad and started to clean the blood off his face. She set a hand on his motion-less arm. "He's freezing."

I spoke. "It's my fault."

She saw the look on my face. "It wasn't your fault. You hit him, but you didn't do this." She shook her head as she assessed his condition. "I think something is really wrong with him."

"No, not that." I stood beside her. "It was my fault Eddy didn't come with us." The secret I had harbored all those years needed to be released. I told Lexie and Mom the truth about that night.

Our ninth birthday. We were excited to finally be almost in double digits. The annual big party was held the day before, so we could head to the cabin on the actual day. Dad's acreage in eastern Washington was huge, with a ten-room log house we called the cabin. We had an RV, too, which we used to drive farther into the wilderness to go camping. Not that an RV was roughing it, but that's what we called camping, anyway.

Gram came with us, sort of. She followed the RV with the

Range Rover. She said she always liked to be prepared for emergencies. Although to her, an emergency might constitute running out of marshmallows for the s'mores we made over the campfire. A trip in the RV wasn't a trip without Gram driving back to the cabin at least once.

As we drove along, Dad told us he had a big surprise for us. And he did. He'd just bought a new two-seater airplane. It went along with the new landing strip in the middle of the property, which is where we went with the RV. It was already dusk when we reached the site, so Dad promised we'd go flying first thing in the morning. We'd flip a coin to see which birthday boy would go first. Of course, I wanted it to be me.

We were getting ready for bed when Eddy started wheezing. Dad discovered a kitten in the RV. Terese admitted to finding it at the cabin, then smuggling it onto the RV. She started to cry and apologized to Eddy. She said she just wanted to make sure the kitten had a home.

The RV medicine cabinet always had some antihistamine for Eddy, but Mom came back empty-handed. "We'd better go get some at the cabin."

Gram volunteered.

Eddy said he felt better. Gram insisted. "Just let me tuck Terese in. I'll take the kitten back to the cabin and get it set up in the garage."

Eddy and I crawled into bed. The airplane ride was still on my mind. "Hey, Eddy. I heard Dad and Gram talking. They said they have another surprise back at the cabin for us. What do you think it is?"

Eddy's eyes widened. He loved surprises.

"Guess we'll have to wait for tomorrow." I rolled over and shut my eyes. I counted on the fact that Eddy also loved a mission.

"Eli? I've got an idea."

"What?" I tried to stop them, but the corners of my mouth wanted to go up.

"I could hop in the back of the Range Rover and go with Gram. I could find out what it is."

I sat up. "That's a great idea. But you have to go now, while she's with Terese."

Eddy opened the window and dropped down to the ground. I lay back, grinning. I knew once Eddy was in the Range Rover with the kitten, he would start wheezing. And Gram would keep driving to the cabin; insist on staying there over-night. I would be the only birthday boy around in the morning when it was time to ride in Dad's new plane.

The rest I didn't plan on: waking up to shouts, the RV moving wildly from side to side, falling out of bed. Then the dark-ness, running blind outside, Dad's shouts telling us which way to turn . . .

But I didn't need to remind Lexie and Mom about that part. They had lived it.

My eyes were full of tears. I couldn't look at my mother or my sister. They were staring at me. I felt their eyes.

Mom's hand touched my arm. I moved away.

"It's done, Eli. And if Eddy were here, you couldn't have contacted him out there. Everyone would still think we were dead."

Lexie didn't say anything to me. She just wiped off the fresh tears finding their way down her face.

Mom's hand caressed my face.

I went to the other side of the room.

She followed.

Both her hands went to my face, holding me. She hadn't been this close to me since I was nine. She smelled of lilacs. Her voice was gentle. "Eli."

Her touch had been only a childhood memory for so long. It was hard for me to believe it was real.

My eyes shut. Hot tears still squeezed out. My head went from side to side. "I'm not . . ."

Mom's grip on my face got stronger. "You're not what, Eli?"

The word came out in a racking sob. "Worthy."

"Oh, Eli. You've always been worthy." She pulled me to her and held me. I let her. "You were a child. Children make mistakes."

My arms went around her. "I'm so sorry." My mouth open against her shoulder, I wept. I wept for Eddy, for what I'd done. So many things I'd done. But mostly, my tears were for the loss of the last six years with my brother.

I wanted them back.

When I stopped blubbering, Mom backed away. Her shoulders straightened as she took a deep breath. Her eyes darkened as they went from me to Lexie and her voice was clear of any fear or sadness. "Let's do what we have to and get out of here."

Mom and Lexie stayed with Dad.

Wiping my face as I ran, I tore down the corridor to his office. As I suspected, it was locked. I could have used Terese's lock-picking skills, but there was no time. At the closest fire extinguisher panel, I broke out the glass and grabbed the axe. Seven whacks later, the office door swung on its hinges.

Once inside, I took a deep breath. I had to find what we needed. I grabbed the phone, hoping for a dial tone. Nothing. How easy that would have been, to just pick up the phone and call out? I imagined that was how he talked to Phil, his accountant. I couldn't think of anyone else he would have trusted with this secret. That guy would probably sell his own internal organs for the right price.

The laptop from Eddy's room was on a shelf. I switched it on, drumming my fingers as I waited for the wireless signal.

Wireless Server Not Available.

I groaned.

It was off. Of course.

Starting with the books on the shelves, I looked everywhere. Book by book, I emptied the shelves and ran my hands over each dusty one. Nothing. The piles of *National Geographic*s ended up on the floor in heaps. I yanked on the drawers of his desk. Locked tight.

I picked up his chair and heaved it at them until they broke open. Papers, notes, lists: proof I was right about everything, but none of it mattered. Nothing gave me the code to the door or the passwords to his computers. I tore the office apart looking for a switch, some way to get on the Internet, the phone, anything. But I kept coming up dry.

I looked over at the door to the secret lab. I couldn't imagine any Internet switch being there. I had to keep moving.

Our only hope was Dad. Maybe he would relent and tell me what I needed to know.

☢

BACK IN THE INFIRMARY, MOM SAT ON THE BED AND LEXIE stood beside her, an arm around her shoulder. Dad's bruised face was clean, and he lay under several layers of blankets, shivering. His eyes were open, but they seemed to be vacant, unfocused. If he noticed me come in, he gave no sign.

Mom looked up at me, her eyebrows raised hopefully. "Any luck?"

I shook my head. "How is he?"

"We took his temperature. It's low."

"That's good, right?" I asked, as I took in what I'd done to his face. Some son.

She shook her head. "No, it's not a good thing. His temperature is low."

"What do you mean by low?"

"Below normal. Below 98.6."

Lexie pulled a blue blanket out of the warmer and we both spread it over Dad. His eyes widened, seemed to focus for a moment. "Oh God." Leaning over the side of the bed, he retched.

Ugh. Turning away, I said, "Got it." I found the mop and bucket in the closet and cleaned up the mess.

Before long Dad had diarrhea, too. He was no more coherent, but we managed to get him to the bathroom. Mom went in with him and shut the door.

Lexie waited for a minute. "I'm gonna go help Terese with the Supp—" She paused. "I mean with the little kids." She left.

I sat down on the edge of the bed, wondering what kind of bug Dad had. How bad he had it. Whether we would all end up with it.

"Eli, are you out there?"

"Yeah, Mom. Right here."

She opened the bathroom door. "He needs to lie down again. Can you help?"

Dad leaned totally on me as we started back to the bed. Suddenly he went limp.

I couldn't hold him.

He dropped to the floor. His head thrashed from side to side. "No!" he screamed. He began to babble, many of the words incoherent.

Mom knelt by him. "Rex? What's wrong?"

Dad seized me by the collar. His breath was hot and stinking in my face. His hands were ice against my skin. "I won't let you do it. I won't." He was agitated, angry, and then he stopped. He fell back on the floor, and then looked up at my mom, pleading. "Clea, don't let them do it."

"Do what, Rex?" She looked as confused as I felt.

"Mom, he's delirious."

Mom sighed. "We've got to find out what's wrong. Maybe we've got medicine for it."

Suddenly Dad seemed to be calm again. Grunting at the effort, I slid him across the floor and lifted him into the bed. I said, "I'll go see what I can find out. You stay here but be careful. If he starts to get violent or seems like he might hurt you, just leave, okay?"

Mom nodded.

In the library, I grabbed several thick medical books. It would have been so much easier to just go on the Internet, find out what I needed. But then I could have gotten us out. I wouldn't have had to play a half-assed doctor.

Back in the room with Dad, Mom and I paged through the reference books. "Mom, what are his symptoms?"

"For weeks now he's been drinking antacid like it's water."

"So . . . heartburn?"

She shook her head. "And the vomiting and diarrhea. Although today may be the first time that's happened."

I frowned. "Those are symptoms for a million things. Let's focus on the unique things."

Mom nodded. "Like his low body temperature."

"Yeah. And being delirious." I kept flipping pages. Then my eyes caught a paragraph about low body temperature. "This couldn't be it."

Mom looked up from the book she held. "What?"

"Well, it lists all those symptoms. Plus seizures, head-aches . . ." I caught my breath. "And itching." I met Mom's stare.

"He's been scratching like crazy."

Reading further, I jammed my finger into the page. "And pins and needles. He said that the other day, that his hands felt like pins and needles."

"Eli, what's the condition?"

I hadn't even looked at that yet. I'd been too busy matching up the symptoms. "Ergotism."

"What is it?"

I kept reading. My heart sunk when I found out what it was. I didn't want to tell my mom.

But she was waiting for me.

I read the definition aloud. "Poisoning by ingesting ergot-infected grains."

Her face registered confusion. She paled as she understood. "The flour."

I scanned a bit more, trying to find out what I could. "There must have been some rye in it that was already infected with the ergot when it came into the Compound."

Her eyes widened. "I . . . I did this."

I started to shake my head, but she grabbed my arm. "I did. But I didn't mean to . . . I just thought . . . I thought it would make him sick, make him weak, so that we all wouldn't have to worry so much about . . ."

"About him doing something crazy?"

She nodded.

We both looked at Dad. He seemed to be asleep. "But it made him crazier."

She looked at me. "Do you think his workers planted the flour?"

I didn't know. "He wouldn't have wanted us to get sick. I really believe that." Too ironic, that he went to the trouble to have someone sabotage the food supply and he was sabotaged himself by the flour.

Mom stood up and walked to the bed. She tucked the blankets in around Dad. "Is there a cure?"

"Yeah. According to this, a derivative of ergot gets used to treat migraines. Once in a while a patient overdoses and they have to treat them for ergotism. Intravenous sodium nitroprusside." Further reading revealed that medicine's own dangers.

"Do we have it?" Mom looked like she was holding her breath.

"Yes." Dad's voice was raspy and weak.

I scratched my head. It was such an obscure medication. "Dad, why would we have that?" Maybe he had planned the ergot poisoning. Why else would he have the antidote?

He swallowed. One of his hands reached up to scratch his face. "I had to have that, of all things. Because of what it becomes if . . . if you take too much."

Mom and I both leaned in, waiting.

"Just in case. In case it came to that for some reason." Dad's eyes had been clear, but then they seemed to glaze over. He recited part of a poem.

> . . . *In this last of meeting places*
> *We grope together*
> *And avoid speech*
> *Gathered on this beach of the tumid river* . . .

The poem was one I knew all too well. I joined him for the next part.

This is the way the world ends
This is the way the world ends
This is the way the world ends
Not with a bang but a whimper.

T. S. Eliot's poem from the beginning of *On the Beach.*

Dad leaned back, trying to catch his breath. He didn't have to tell me more. I understood why he had sodium nitroprusside. I explained to Mom. "Too much of it gives you cyanide poisoning."

Mom gasped. "But that's deadly."

I nodded. "That's the point."

Dad's voice was weak. "Can't survive a nuclear war without cyanide."

Among everything else, my dad turned out to be a walking cliché.

I sighed. "Mom, do you know how to put in an IV?"

"No."

Pity they didn't cover *that* at the commune.

I leaned in. "Dad. You've got to give me the code for the door. Let me go out and get you help. You have to or you're going to die."

He nodded. "Yes. Yes. The code. Of course. We must have the code." His eyes were strange again, not clear.

I could tell there wasn't much behind them. "Dad, if you just hold on. Please, just hold on, stay with me. Can you tell me the code?"

He grabbed my hand.

I wanted to pull away. I tried.

But his grip was so strong. His eyes cleared again. "Eli. I'm sorry. I'm sorry for everything."

It was a little late. Maybe it would be enough to get him to give me the code. "Dad, can you tell me the code? Please, that will make up for everything." Not quite, but it would be a decent start.

His lips formed the words. "The numbers . . ."

I squeezed his hand even harder than he was squeezing mine. "Tell me the numbers."

He started to recite numbers, so many numbers they blended into each other. "Nineteen . . . four . . . five . . . eight . . . six . . ."

"Dad, wait . . . Mom! I need pen and paper!"

Mom started ripping open drawers, searching.

"Eight . . . two . . . nine . . ." He kept on with the numbers, so many they didn't even begin to start sinking in. Like a phone number from hell.

"Dad, please! Hold on, I can't remember them all."

Mom was still banging drawers. "I can't find anything to write with!"

Dad squeezed my hand again. "Son—"

I paused, leaning over him. My hair cascaded in front of my face and I pushed it aside. "Dad, I'm here."

The corners of his mouth turned up slightly. "You can save them. You can."

I breathed out, not knowing if he was right or not. I hoped he was. "I know, Dad. You'll give me the numbers and I'll get us out."

He started again, reciting numbers, so fast that I wanted to scream.

The numbers stopped. Dad began to convulse, his limbs thrashing.

"Mom!"

She ran to my side. Together, we tried to hold him down as his whole body jerked.

Before it got so bad that he passed out, he managed to spit out one word.

"Turducken."

CHAPTER SEVENTEEN

DAD WAS STILL AND UNRESPONSIVE. MOM AND I LOOKED AT each other.

I rubbed my chin. "Do you know anything? Did Dad ever say anything about this?"

She put her hand over her mouth. "Early on, I asked your father once, about the code to the door. How we would get out if something happened to him. Of course he said nothing would happen to him. Still, he promised he would leave a way for us to get out."

I wasn't sure how much weight a promise from my father carried anymore. "But he went crazy since then. He didn't want us to leave."

Mom met my eyes. She hesitated.

I wanted to grab her shoulders and shake, anything to get the words to come out faster. "Mom? What?"

She looked down at her belly as she rubbed it. "He told me he'd leave a clue. That there was a clue that would lead to another and another, eventually leading to the answer."

"So that's it. Turducken must be the clue."

Mom let out a breath. "That wasn't all. The first time he told me about it, he was still nice. He acted like it was just matter-of-fact, a little scavenger hunt. Then, later, when he started to get mean . . ."

"Mom?"

"I was afraid he would go back on his word. But then he laughed, said he would leave the clue, even though he didn't think any of us would be able to figure it out."

I looked at Dad, lying in the bed. "I think he's sorry for it. For everything. And he wants us to get out. Maybe it's just to save himself, but it doesn't matter." I sighed. "I need to think. To figure this out."

Mom nodded. "Why don't you take some time?"

"No, I need to—"

Reaching over Dad, she grabbed my hand. "Take some time. Even just a half hour. I'll stay here."

I tried to protest.

"Promise me. You don't come back here for thirty minutes."

I promised.

Despite everything that had just happened, I was hungry. On my way to the kitchen, I heard giggles coming from one of the rooms. The salon. Inside, Lexie was trimming the little girl's hair.

How could she be doing that when our world was ripping apart? I stepped closer, planning to give her hell.

Lexie told the little girl to sit still, and said her name. Cara.

Cara sat in a booster seat on the swivel chair, smiling at herself in the mirror. Lexie's eyes met mine in our reflections.

My mouth opened, ready to yell, ask her how she could just be standing there like nothing was wrong.

She saw the look in my eyes. "They don't know anything." Her eyes drifted down to Cara. "They don't know about worry or sadness. All they know is that life is simple and secure and every day will be like the one before it." She looked back at me. "That's a gift. Do you want to be the one responsible for taking it away?"

I leaned against the doorway, my throat tight.

"You're done, sweetie." Lexie helped Cara get down and led her over to some blocks, then came over to me and spoke so Cara couldn't hear. "What's going on?"

I told her the truth. "I'm not sure."

"Then I'm going to keep helping with the little kids. It's my routine and routine is good." Lexie went in front of the mirror and took out her bun, letting her hair cascade around her shoulders. She combed through it and started to trim.

My eyes went to my reflection in the mirror. My own hair. I pulled it forward and let it cover my face so I could no longer see. As I pushed it back, my fingers ran through it. My hair was my shield, a wall, to keep everyone out. Or was it? Did it keep something in? My reflection smiled a bit. I had no secrets left. "Want to cut mine?"

Lexie stopped trimming. "Are you kidding me?"

I shook my head.

"You trust me to cut your hair?"

"Hell, no." I smiled.

"Then . . ."

"It could use a trim." I sat down in the chair. "And I have thirty minutes to kill. Mom's orders."

Lexie set down the scissors and picked up a wide-toothed comb. She hesitated, and then began.

My hair was thick, hard to comb through. "Ow."

"Sorry." She stopped.

"I'm used to it."

She finished combing and started to cut, barely taking off more than an inch. She paused. "Can I ask you something?"

"I'm kind of at your mercy right now, so go ahead." In my lap, my fingers were wringing the hair band as my knuckles turned white.

"What do you remember of me, from before? When we didn't live here?" She started cutting again.

"Grapes."

"Huh?"

"Frozen grapes. I hated to watch you eat them, it was like someone scratching a blackboard."

Lexie smiled. "I loved frozen grapes. The way the cold almost hurt." She shook her head. "I miss them. I was mad that Dad couldn't even throw some in the freezers down here."

I didn't say anything.

She just stood there. "It wasn't even that. You know what bothered me?"

I shrugged.

"That maybe he didn't stock any because he had no idea they were my favorite food. That's what really bothered me."

"There's a lot Dad didn't know about all of us. And even more we didn't know about him."

Lexie kept cutting.

I grabbed her arm. "Wait."

"What?" She looked at me in the mirror. "You wanted me to do this. Is it too short?"

I let her go and stood up, pulling out drawers until I found what I was looking for. I brandished the electric clippers. "Use these."

"I can't trim hair with those."

"Don't want it trimmed." I handed her the clippers and sat back down. "I want it gone."

"Why?"

There wasn't an explanation I could put into words. "Just do it."

The buzzing started.

She didn't shave my head, but adjusted the setting to give me a short cut. The hair fell off in long clumps, drifting to the floor.

When the buzzing stopped, I ran my hands over my scalp.

I felt lighter. Less burdened. And totally visible to anyone who wanted to see me.

"You look good." Lexie smiled. "Definitely an improvement, anyway."

When I stood, I was ankle deep in my own hair.

"Go." Lexie took the broom from the corner. "I'll clean it up."

"Thanks."

On the way to the kitchen for a quick salad, I heard a bang from the direction of Dad's office. Mom was inside the secret lab, tearing it apart. Shattered glass lay everywhere. Before I could stop her, she shoved over a table with a grunt, spilling piles of papers on the floor.

"Mom!"

She turned to look at me, her chest heaving. Her hair had come loose and a few strands hung down in front of her face. "I have to find that clue and get you all out of here."

She noticed my hair then, and started to say something else, then fell backward, grabbing for something to hold on to. She could only reach a small stand, which toppled onto her as she collapsed on the floor, unconscious, in a small pool of blood.

CHAPTER EIGHTEEN

I FLEW ACROSS THE ROOM, TOSSING ASIDE THE STAND AND sending it clattering to the other side of the room. Mom lay on the floor.

"Mom?"

I put one arm under her legs and the other around her waist, scooping her up in my arms. Her body flopped against mine as I carried her to the infirmary and laid her down on the bed next to Dad's.

I dug around for smelling salts and waved them under her nose.

Her eyelids fluttered. "I don't feel so well."

My efforts to get her to sit didn't work. She groaned and lay back down.

"Mom, what hurts?"

Mom licked her lips. "My stomach. Really bad cramps." She rolled a bit with the pain.

"You're bleeding." I grabbed some extra sheets and

towels from the linen closet and spread them under her on the bed as best as I could.

She lay propped up on some pillows, holding her stomach. "Ohhhh." Her face was pale.

"You shouldn't have done that. I'll find the clue." My words spoke what I wanted to be feeling, but I wasn't. All I could think was that she had to be okay, I couldn't do it without her. I could not be responsible for all of us. I wasn't up to it.

Not even thinking, I reached to loosen my hair, put up my wall. But my hand found only the back of my head, which was covered with soft prickles.

I held my open hand in front of my eyes. My wall was gone. It didn't matter whether I felt up to the task or not. Our lives depended on me. My fingers curled into a tight fist before releasing.

"Mom?"

Her eyes shut. "Hurts."

My hand touched her arm. "Cramps?"

"No." She grimaced. "Worse."

It was crucial to figure out for sure what was wrong with Mom before I would know how to help. If I could. By paging through the index of one of the medical books, I found what I was looking for. I quickly scanned through descriptions of pregnancy complications.

Mom sighed. "I know what it is, Eli. I had it with Terese."

I looked at my mother. "What happened?"

Her eyebrows rose. "Nothing. They put me on bed rest."

As I glanced over at Dad, I noticed a syringe on the bed-side table. A small bottle of the sodium nitroprusside sat beside it. I picked it up. Empty.

"Mom?"

She looked at the bottle in my hand and raised her eye-brows a bit. "I had to try. He may be our only way out."

Lexie walked in. She rushed to Mom's side as soon as she saw her face.

I explained what was going on. Then I looked at Mom. "So you'll stay in bed until I get us out of here."

She tried to get up. "I need to . . ."

With a gentle touch, Lexie pushed her back. "No, we can do it. I'll help Terese with the babies. I already told her Dad was sick. I'll tell her you're just . . . just hanging out with him and getting some rest." Lexie looked at me. "And Eli will figure out how to get us out of here."

She was the last person I expected to be confident in my abilities as a savior.

Before she left, Lexie kissed Mom on the cheek. And she whispered to me, "*Can* you get us out of here?" She didn't wait for an answer.

Mom stared at the ceiling. "This puts a kink in things."

"No, we'll take care of everything, really. You need to lie still."

She sighed. "Eli? I like your haircut."

I picked up her hand and held it between both of mine. Although touching someone still felt like a struggle, so strange after so long without the sensation, it was becoming more normal. Maybe I needed to get used to it. If we got out of here, we would all have to get used to normal again, whatever that might be. Normal again, to me, would be to touch someone, without having to summon up courage.

"Mom, what did the doctors say when this happened before?"

She didn't answer right away. "It wasn't that big a deal, really."

"Did they tell you it could happen again?"

"Yes."

"And that wasn't a problem?"

"Even on bed rest, there was a chance it could have been bad enough that they would have to do an emergency C-section. That's what they told me. They also said . . ."

"What? What did they say?"

Mom leaned back again. "Because I was getting a bit older, they recommended that Terese be my last baby."

I felt my heart in my throat. "Did Dad know that?"

"Of course."

"And he let you have more babies? Down here, with no doctors?" I didn't need the answer.

She shut her eyes.

I covered her with a blanket and left, careful to be quiet as I closed the door.

Out in the hall, I leaned against the wall for support. I had to figure out what *turducken* meant. Was it the clue? I needed to find out. Fast.

For the first time in six years, I did not have all the time in the world.

CHAPTER NINETEEN

Turducken.

I tried it as a password in the computers. Even tried to figure out a numeric code that might be attached to the sequenced letters, starting with the basics: each letter's position in the alphabet.

Nothing. Everything I tried seemed too easy.

I knew what I had to do. Terese and Lexie were in the kitchen, eating. "Reese, we have to tell you something."

Lexie looked at me with wide eyes, shaking her head.

Terese looked from one of us to the other.

Lexie spoke first. "Mom's not feeling well. She's in bed for a few days."

Terese's eyes widened and she set down her fork. "Is she okay?"

I tried to keep my voice upbeat. "Yeah, she'll be fine. We're going to get her help soon."

Terese's eyes narrowed and the corners of her mouth turned down. "You're lying to me."

If I was ever going to prove I wasn't just out for myself, I needed to start somewhere. "We aren't lying."

Lexie waved her hand from behind Terese, trying to get my attention.

I ignored her.

Lexie's shoulders slumped.

I continued, "Reese, we aren't lying, just not telling you everything. I got through to Eddy on the Internet. At least I think I did."

She just stared at me.

"Reese, you were right. About everything. Eddy is fine. Gram, too. It's a long story. They thought we were dead all these years. They're going to try to find us. Try to get us out."

"Father did it." She didn't even blink. She just knew.

That jolted me a bit. "Yeah."

"I told you so."

"Yeah, you did. I'm sorry I didn't believe you. Truly sorry." I put a hand on her arm.

Her eyes slowly tracked to my hand on her arm.

I moved my hand away from her. I didn't remember the last time I'd touched her. Maybe I never had.

She looked up at me. "Can we go home?"

"I hope so." I forced a grin. "And now we need your help. We have to find the code for the door in order to get out, okay? I think I found a clue. I mean, Dad actually told me this word and I think it might be the clue."

Lexie wiped her chin on her shoulder. "What's the clue?"

"Turducken."

Lexie spoke up. "Didn't we have that for Christmas one year?"

"Yeah, it was great." My mouth watered.

"No, it was disgusting." Lexie pushed her plate away. "Dad made me eat a piece, ugh."

"Do you remember anything about it?"

Lexie didn't say anything, but her shoulders rose slightly.

Terese took a drink of water, spilling some.

I dug around in one of the drawers. My knuckles were sore and I remembered seeing a bottle of ibuprofen. "I tried to piece together a password on his computers, nothing worked." I found the bottle. Totally expired. I swallowed two, anyway.

Lexie looked at me. "Now what?"

I hopped up to sit on the counter. "Don't know. Any ideas?"

Terese wiped her eyes. Her voice was meek. "Do you think the word is supposed to trigger something? Make you think of something else that is the code?"

I made an attempt to encourage her, which was not something I was experienced at. "That might be true. Good thinking." At least it sounded sincere to me.

Lexie groaned. "Why are we even trying to figure this out? *Hello.* Dad is a brainiac, for cripes' sake. I mean, despite everything, he's still way smarter than you, Eli. Can't we wait for him to get better and just tell us the code?"

"Mom and Dad need medical help that we don't have. We can't wait."

"Does he truly want us to figure it out?" Terese looked skeptical.

For a moment I glanced at Lexie. "Of course he does. So please, try to think of anything at all that might help. Even if it seems stupid. Let me know, okay?"

Terese nodded and stood up. "They'll be waking up from their naps soon," she said. "I'll check on them."

Lexie went with me to check on Mom and Dad. "I'll stay with them, Eli." They were both asleep.

I needed to think. And I did my best thinking when I ran.

On the treadmill, I focused. Turducken, that long-ago Christmas, what did I remember? Everything, I needed to remember everything.

Free association.

A chicken inside a duck inside a turkey.

A turkey stuffed with a duck stuffed with a chicken.

Poultry, game bird, water fowl, webbed feet, rooster, hen, drake, mallard.

Nothing. I had nothing.

I got off the treadmill and held my hands over my head, catching my breath. I'd run more than eight miles.

"Eli." Lexie beckoned from the door. "I may have thought of something."

I walked over to where she stood with her arms crossed.

"What?"

"I'm not sure." She leaned against the wall. "Maybe it's nothing . . ."

I wiped my face with my sleeve and forced myself to wait, silent.

"I'd just gotten home for Christmas vacation when those things came."

"Turduckens."

"Yes. I'd missed lunch to take a final, and then with the ride home I was starved, so I went in the kitchen to ask Els to make me a sandwich or something. Dad was there. We just got to talking, because I hadn't seen him since Thanksgiving. And he was so excited when they started carrying in those turduckens. I asked him why he was so excited about a bunch of turkeys and he said, 'These have a surprise inside.'"

"That's it?"

She shrugged a little. "Sorry."

"No, I wasn't being mean, Lex, honest. It may help."

"Right." She left.

I stripped off my sweaty shirt and dropped to the floor to stretch.

Lexie came back in. "I'm wrong."

"About what?"

"What he said. It wasn't, there's a surprise, it was . . . Oh, now I remember, because he said it in a silly voice, like a French accent. I remember because he never did that, acted silly. He said, '*Eeets* not just a turkey. There *eees* a *meesstery* inside.'" She waited. "Hello, I remembered. Does it help?"

I didn't answer. My mind was whirling. *A mystery inside.* So familiar. I'd heard that recently. But where? And when?

A mystery inside.

Those words ate me up. For the next hour, I sequestered myself in Dad's office and looked through everything I could find in the papers, books, CDs. Even some of the *National Geographic*s. Nothing struck a chord.

I gave up. Had to. I was driving myself crazy.

Out in the hall, I ran into Terese. For the first time ever, her hair was down, not in pigtails. Her eyes were red. She put her head down and tried to walk right by me. "What's wrong?"

She didn't answer. But I knew. She was scared.

Something else about her was different. "Reese, I know you're upset about Mom and Dad. We haven't even given you a chance to deal; we're just shoving all this on you." I knelt, so that I looked up at her. "I know I've been a crappy brother lately—"

She wiped her eyes. "You've always been a crappy brother."

Her accent was gone.

"Okay, fine. I've always been a crappy brother. But I'm here now, okay? For whatever you need." I figured it out. Why she looked different. She wasn't in purple. Instead, she wore black. That and having her hair down made her look older. No. Not older. Just her own age for once.

Funny. The Compound had a way of making me feel older than I was. I'd felt like an adult since I was nine. But the Compound seemed to have done the opposite to Terese. She'd stayed the same, perhaps even regressed. Maybe she felt a change coming. So she felt *she* had to change, too.

"Want to go to Dad's office with me?"

She nodded.

In the office she was quiet, just leaning against the door and looking around. "Why do you call me Little Miss Perfect?"

Embarrassed, I stammered. "You are, like, perfect. You always do the right thing and say the right thing and everyone loves you for it."

"No." She paused. "Not everyone."

"Huh?"

"Lexie doesn't love me. Neither do you."

"Yes, she does. She just doesn't show it."

She waited a moment. "And you, Eli? Do you love me?"

"Of course, you're my sister."

"But you don't like me. And that's worse than not being loved." She started to leave.

"Reese, wait."

She turned back.

I looked at my feet, stalling. "Honestly, I've had a hard time here without Eddy. I was closer to him than anyone. And you, you're a lot like him." I took a deep breath. "I hated that you were here and he wasn't." Even though it was my fault he wasn't there, I had blamed her. "It was always the situation, not you. You're my little sister. Yeah. I do like you."

One of her shoulders went up and down. "You know, you're not that bad a brother."

"Really?" I wanted to know.

"There's still a chance for you, anyway." She smiled a tiny bit. "Want to go see the babies with me?"

I'd been cooped up in the office for hours; maybe new scenery would give me a fresh perspective. Or maybe I was trying to live up to my new status as not-so-crappy-brother-after-all. "Just for a while. I've got to get back to Mom and Dad."

In the nursery, Lucas and Cara romped. They threw beanbags at each other while Quinn played in the playpen.

Lucas skipped over to me. "Play with us, 'kay?"

"Yeah."

Then it hit me. Lucas had said those words. *The mystery inside.* The first day I came to their room. "Lucas!"

"What?"

"Come here a sec." I whispered in his ear, "Can you show me your clown, remember, that you showed me before?"

" 'Kay. They can't see, though." Lucas's eyes darted to Cara and Quinn.

"Sure." He led me to the closet. The clown came out from the hiding place.

"You'll be careful?"

I liked listening to him, to his nearly five-year-old diction. "Yeah."

Piece by piece, I took the clowns apart, setting them down until I held the inner clown.

Shaking produced nothing but silence.

Close inspection revealed no secret notches or buttons.

Then I read the word written on the bottom again. At first, I had assumed it was only the manufacturer, but perhaps . . .

"Hey, Reese, come here."

Lucas tried to grab the clown from me. "Don't let her see!"

I held it out of his reach. "Lucas, it's okay."

She came into the closet. "What're you guys doing in here?"

"Reese, is this French?" Over Lucas's head, I handed her the smallest clown.

Squinting, she read the word. *"Hautbois."*

Lucas kept trying to grab it back.

I pushed him out of the way. "Reese, what does it mean?"

"Translated? High wood."

I groaned. Talk about cryptic. "Thanks." I took the clown back, wondering what to do next.

Terese started to leave, then stopped. "Is that something to do with the code?"

Lucas took the clown from my hand.

I shook my head. "I thought it was, but it doesn't make any sense."

Terese shrugged. "I guess not. What would my oboe have to do with it?"

My heart jumped. "What?"

"Hautbois, high wood. That's where the word *oboe* comes from."

I tried to keep my voice calm as I grabbed her arm. Touching people seemed more normal all the time. "Is your oboe in the music room?"

She nodded.

I raced out of there. In the music room, Terese's oboe was on its stand. I took it apart and scrutinized every section. *A mystery inside.* Did that refer to the clown or the oboe? What?

The case caught my eye. I brushed the parts aside and focused my attention on the case. Solid, sturdy, the case had probably cost a lot of money, too. That wasn't a priority as I tore into it, ripping out the lining. The case was empty, nothing. I kicked the pile of lining nearest to my left foot. A piece of paper fluttered out. Between my fingers, the item felt more like parchment. The paper was blank.

"No, no, no."

With the parchment firmly in my grip, I left the room and went to the kitchen. I sat in the nook, the paper on the table in front of me. I tried to figure out the reasoning for it all. Dad telling me the word *turducken.*

Which led to Lexie remembering *the mystery inside.*

Which led to Lucas and the nesting dolls, obviously a present from Dad.

From there, *hautbois,* which led to Terese's oboe.

We had all played our part. Hadn't we? Was that my role, to put it together?

I looked at the parchment. Was this also meant for me to figure out?

As I flipped the parchment over and over, something occurred to me. When we were eight, Eddy and I had been into playing spy games. Dad gave us invisible ink and we wrote secret messages. But that was from a kit I didn't have anymore.

Something else came to mind. A chemistry lesson Dad had done with me. You could make an ink. Out of what?

I carried the parchment into the lab. I remembered: phenolphthalein. And that it could be revealed by something. Damn, I couldn't remember. Vapors, some kind of vapors.

In the lab, I scanned the shelves of chemicals, hoping something would ring a bell. It had to be something simple, everyday, right? If it was too complicated, Dad risked me not ever figuring it out. He did want me to figure it out, didn't he?

No. Of course he didn't.

Even if I had figured out the first clue, *turducken*, he wouldn't have expected me to go to Lexie, who would provide the next part. And Lucas and the nesting clowns. They were a present from Dad. He knew I wouldn't go to the nursery.

And Terese. He knew what I called her, how I didn't like to be around her. He relied on my own predictability to keep me from finding the answer. I didn't get along with my sisters enough to get their cooperation.

He counted on me being the same selfish, detached, untouchable loner I had been ever since we entered the Compound. Living behind my wall, not letting anything out. Or anyone in.

What else had he counted on me doing? Or not doing?

There was a plastic tote of cleaners sitting nearby. I fiddled with the bottle of glass cleaner, thinking how my father yelled at Mom and the girls if the lab wasn't spotless.

I paused.

Behind the bottle of glass cleaner, there was a container of bleach. I stared at it for a moment, then felt myself actually grinning. "Yes!" Ammonia fumes. Ammonia fumes revealed the phenolphthalein ink.

Donning a face mask and gloves, I went to work with a beaker of ammonia. I held the parchment over the beaker. "Please, please, please."

A message slowly revealed itself. Numbers. Lots of numbers, over two dozen.

The code?

What else could it be?

I had it. I had the power to get us out of here.

Someone clapped hands behind me, in a slow rhythm. I turned.

My father stood there, leaning against the doorjamb, still clapping slowly. "Well done, Eli. I'm impressed."

His face was raw and bruised. "Dad! Are you okay?"

He shrugged a bit. "Oh, fine. Fine as anyone can be when HIS WIFE IS TRYING TO POISON HIM!"

His shout made me jump. I took a step back, picking up the parchment as I moved. Had he done something to Mom? "She didn't know, she just wanted you to have bread and—"

He held up a hand to silence me. His face was sweaty

but he didn't seem shaky. Exactly the opposite. "So you have the code now."

I nodded. "We can get out, get you some help . . ."

"I don't need ANY HELP!"

Again, his shout made me jump. I clutched the code in my palm.

He took a step inside the door.

I had to get out, away from him, and try the code. Me getting out was our only chance.

Dad let out a loud ragged sigh. "You try to do everything for your family, and what do they do in return?"

I sensed it was a rhetorical question.

"They try and *poison* you." He picked up a Bunsen burner and slammed it on the floor for effect. I used the distraction to take a step toward the door, even as he moved slowly away from it, looking for something else to throw.

"I gave you everything. Everything . . ." He started picking up anything in his reach and hurled each item as he spoke. "Everything." A tray of test tubes hit the ground. "Everything." A pile of petri dishes hit the near wall, glass flying. *"Everything."*

When he used both hands to pick up a microscope, I took my chance and ran out of the room as fast as I could.

I heard a roar behind me as he realized I was gone.

I shoved the parchment in my pocket and ran toward the door, my arms pumping. My heart pounded, more from the last few minutes than the physical exertion. At the hallway to the infirmary, I paused. I wanted to make sure Mom was okay. Make sure he hadn't hurt her. But the only way to truly help her was to open that door and get help.

"Eli?" Dad's faint voice from behind me spurred me on.

I ran down the hall, into the family room, and through the archway.

The corridor seemed shorter than I remembered, because all too soon the silver door stood before me. In the surface, my face was reflected. Despite the distortion, I could still see my terrified expression. I saw myself there, in the door, clutching the parchment.

Yes, I was scared.

More than that, I was ready. Ready to do it, to try the code.

The silver door had a panel with a keypad. So simple. Yes, so simple, if you had the code.

I prayed that I did. I prayed so hard.

I hoped God was still around to hear.

I had to stop and think for a minute, to breathe. My hands shook. There might be a security lock as well, something that shut down the system if any wrong numbers were pushed. I took a few precious moments to breathe deep, try to calm myself. I couldn't risk hitting a wrong number. Not when I was almost there.

"You're so close, Eli."

I gasped, whipping around to see my father.

He smiled, his hands behind his back. "This is such a big occasion, you shouldn't be all alone."

One of his arms slowly came around, revealing that it

was wrapped around Lucas, who looked up at me, confusion all over his face.

"Eli?"

I looked from him to Dad and shook my head, panic rising in my chest. "Let him go!"

Dad's smile only widened as he gripped Lucas by the shoulders. "Let him go?" He leaned down and spoke to Lucas. "You want to go with Eli, right?"

Lucas nodded, looking surer of himself.

Dad straightened up. "He wants to go."

I didn't know what to do.

"Lucas, remember that song I taught you?"

Lucas nodded again.

"Do you think you can cover your ears and sing that song at the same time?"

Lucas grinned. "I think so."

"Go ahead."

With his small hands, Lucas reached up and covered his ears. Then, his voice, quiet at first, began to sing, *"I am Enery the Eighth I am, Enery the Eighth I am I am . . ."* His voice got louder as he kept singing. But it wasn't loud enough to drown out my father's words.

"What do you think, Eli?" His hands moved up to my brother's throat as he spoke. "Should I choke the life out of him?" His hands moved farther up. "Or just snap his neck. That would be quicker."

My head went from side to side. "Don't." Despite trying to stay calm, the word was a plea. "Please don't."

"It's your choice. I just need that." His eyes went to the paper in my hand.

Lucas was back at the chorus again, singing louder, a worried look on his face.

"Eli, time to choose."

I glanced at the paper again, wondering how many of the numbers I could memorize before—

"NOW!"

I jumped. So did Lucas, who stopped singing. He tried to wriggle away from Dad's grasp, but he couldn't.

"Choose, Eli."

I could chance it. Lucas was his child, he wouldn't hurt him. But then I looked into my father's eyes, only they were no longer my father's. They belonged to a madman.

Lucas looked up at me and whimpered, his eyes wet.

My knees nearly buckled as I stepped forward, holding out the paper. "Here! Take it! Let him go!"

Dad released Lucas as he reached out for the code and took it from me. "Good choice, son. Very unselfish." With the paper still in his hand, he gave me a casual salute, then left.

I knelt down in front of Lucas. "Are you okay?"

Lucas nodded as he sniffled. "That was scary."

My arms went around him and he leaned into me. "I know. I was scared, too."

My father's footsteps receded down the hall.

I leaned back, looking into my brother's face. "But now we have to be brave, okay? We have work to do."

Lucas wiped his nose with his sleeve. "What kinda work?"

I glanced over at the door. "I've gotta figure out some numbers." I stood back up and took his hand. "Come on."

CHAPTER TWENTY

I WANTED TO GO CHECK ON MOM, BUT I DIDN'T DARE. I HAD no idea what Dad was planning, and I knew my time was short. My only chance was to figure out the code using the few numbers I remembered. If it could be figured out. I had to try. Getting out was the only true way to help my mother.

Lexie and Terese were with the little kids. Once Lucas and I were inside, I dragged a dresser in front of the door.

Lexie walked over to me and whispered, "What's going on?"

I glanced at the others, but they seemed occupied. "I had the code, but Dad stopped me."

"How? He's too sick."

"Well, he got better real frickin' fast." I lowered my voice. "Threatened to hurt Lucas if I didn't give him the paper with the code."

Lexie's jaw clenched.

"What about Mom?"

"I don't know. He may be there. He could be anywhere. I have to figure this thing out."

Lexie frowned. "I thought he took the code back."

"He did, but I remember a few of the numbers. They have to mean something; it's just a matter of putting it together." I glanced over at a kiddie chalkboard. "I need your help."

With a piece of chalk, I wrote down the few numbers I remembered.

5_____5716____89

Lexie stared at the chalkboard. "That's it? How many numbers in the code total?"

"Way more. At least two dozen."

She breathed out. "Man."

"Yeah."

Lexie thought for a bit. "You're sure about these, though?"

I nodded. "I'm not sure how many numbers in between, but I know these are in the right order. Sort of."

Terese came over and I told her what we were doing.

"Are they all separate numbers?"

I looked at her. "Why?"

She put a slash on the board.

5_____57/16____89

"July sixteenth, that's your birthday."

My mouth dropped open.

She shrugged. "Maybe it's all our birthdays?"

She put some more numbers on the board.

11/17

"That's Lexie."

I shook my head. "Those weren't in it, I'm pretty sure."

Terese bit her lip. "So it's not our birthdays."

As I erased the ones she'd put up, I gazed at the others.
So, 7/16 was a date, a date other than my birthday.

5_____57/16___89

I added more numbers.

5_____57/161945__89

Lexie leaned in. "What's that?"

"Date they set off the atomic bomb at the Trinity test site."

"Nifty. So what are the rest?"

"Oh my God." Slowly I erased the slash and filled in
other numbers. Then I stepped back to read the result.

5_____5716194586194589194 5

"Holy crap, that's it."

Lexie was by my side, looking at the board. "You've
got it?"

"Part of it." I pointed. "These are dates of nuclear bomb explosions. Trinity test site, July 16, 1945. Then Hiroshima, August 6, 1945. Nagasaki, August 9, 1945."

"Wow." Lexie and Terese spoke together.

I rubbed my eyes. "But that's not all of it. What else is there?"

Lexie pointed at the first number. "So if they're all dates, what happened in May?"

"May? Nothing happened in May, they didn't even . . ." I trailed off as something flashed in my memory. There had been a test, before July 16. A pretest explosion. It didn't really count, but could that be it? I wrote in the numbers and hoped I had the date right.

571945716194586194589194 5

I smiled. "It looks right. No way of knowing for sure, but it all looks familiar."

Terese patted my shoulder. "So that's it?"

"No. There were more numbers."

Lexie sighed. "Another date?"

"Probably. There were so many other tests, though. Which date is the one?"

Lexie sat down on the floor. "Isn't this all ironic? That the code is all about nuclear war, the entire reason this place was built?"

I shrugged. "These dates aren't really about nuclear war per se, because they're all bombs built by the same

218

country, and a nuclear war would be bombs from at least
two countries, which . . ."

"What?"

My hand went to my mouth. "Lexie, you're right."

"What?"

"The last date." I put in the numbers.

571945716194586194589194582919 49

Terese considered the numbers. "What happened August 29, 1949?"

I smiled. "The first Soviet nuclear detonation." I looked at Lexie. "There's your reason for the Compound." I grabbed a piece of paper and pen, jotted the numbers down, double-checking them three times, then handed them off to Lexie to check as well.

"Do you think that's it?" Lexie sounded hopeful.

"One way to find out."

"Can I go?" Lucas stood in front of me.

I set a hand on his shoulder. "Oh, buddy, I need to go fast."

He stuck out his foot, showing me his cross trainers just like mine. "I can go fast."

He felt scrawny under my grip. "I'll come back for you, okay? But now I have to leave." I shoved aside the dresser. "Lexie, make sure you put this back after I leave."

She stepped over to me, hesitated, and then gave me a quick hug. "Good luck," she whispered. *"Hurry."*

Again, I found myself running down the hall, into the family room, and through the archway.

This time I didn't hesitate. My right index finger punched in the numbers. A series of electronic blips sounded. With a loud puff of air, the vacuum seal of the door released. The silver door fell open. Stale air came through.

"Thank you, God."

I grabbed an edge and pushed the door out of my way. Other than being dusty, the entryway to the stairs was in pretty much the same condition as I'd last seen it six years before.

It seemed smaller. And dimmer. A lone red emergency light lit the area. There was a fuse box on the wall. I opened it and started flipping switches. One flooded the area with light.

I started to climb the stairs two at a time. All that money and Dad couldn't invest in an elevator? I suppose he thought about what fifteen years without maintenance would do to the machinery and figured stairs were a better idea.

As I climbed the metal stairs, my footsteps were quiet. I thought they should make more noise. The way down had been so loud and chaotic. Maybe I expected that from the trip back up as well.

After two flights, my breaths came faster. I didn't remember the trip being so arduous the first time. But this trip I was climbing, not descending.

I found myself thinking of the first rainy day of second

grade. I was anxious to wear my new blue slicker with matching boots. As always, Mom drove us, me and Eddy in the middle seats.

We stopped for her coffee at Tully's, the smell of it filling the SUV as we turned into the school driveway. We sat in a line of other cars as they idled at the entrance and gently ejected their small passengers. Vivaldi played on the radio and the heater blew warm air, pleasantly overheating us.

Waiting our turn, I adjusted my backpack and got a better grip on my blue lunchbox, which held the same thing every day, packed by Els. Peanut butter sandwich, decrusted and cut diagonally into fourths. Minicarrots. A snack bag of chocolate chip cookies. They came with a napkin and a sweet, tender note from my mom, ending always with

ILY Eli! Mommy.

The SUV moved up. We popped open the doors. Mom blew kisses and waved good-bye. We shrieked, jumping boot first into the downpour, ecstatic to be seven years old on a rainy day.

I wanted that again. That security that came from knowing exactly what was in my lunchbox. I wanted that so bad.

At the top of the stairs, I saw the hatch. I didn't remember it being so wide, but then I basically got shoved down it the first time. There hadn't been a lot of time for observation. A skinny set of steps ascended and I took them nearly in one leap.

I pushed on the hatch. Didn't budge. I panicked, thinking maybe Dad had Phil or someone seal us in.

Driven by adrenaline, I shoved with my hands as hard as I could. I felt it loosen a tiny bit, enough for a little dirt to dribble in around the edge. I relaxed. Soil had probably accumulated over the opening. Maybe we weren't trapped. My fingers reached through, pushing dirt out of the way, pulling some of it inside. I still couldn't garner enough leeway to get my hand out to work away the rest of the dirt.

Once more I strained, shoving my hand out the slim opening. The hatch didn't move any more. I tried to pull my hand back in.

It was stuck. Stuck in the cookie jar of the outside world.

"No, no, *no*!"

If I yelled for help, would my family hear me?

"Crap!"

Someone grabbed my leg. "Need a hand?"

I didn't even have a chance to look at my father before he started yanking me downward, out of the hatch.

"No!!" My hand was stuck, and his violent wrenching was going to break my wrist. "Stop!" I kicked out with my legs as I tried to anchor myself up.

Dad was almost breathless as he kept on trying to pull me out. "Did I surprise you? Because you sure as hell surprised me, figuring out the code like that."

Each comment was emphasized by a hard yank, each one making me want to scream out in pain.

"How'd you do it? Memorize the numbers? There was maybe enough time, maybe enough time, but I didn't think so, a lot of numbers to remember, the human mind can really only process seven at a time, that's why phone numbers are seven digits long . . ."

The pain in my wrist got so bad I couldn't follow his rambling. I tried to kick out at him. "Stop! Stop it!" My cries echoed in the space as I tried to concentrate. Tried to plan. No one was going to save me. He was hurting me. There was only one way to make it stop. I looked down at him the best I could, waiting for the right moment.

"You know how I figured it out, Dad?"

He paused to look up at me, like he really wanted to know.

"You taught me well." I stood on my left leg and flailed out with my right foot as hard as I could. I felt it connect with his face, so I did it again, finding even more strength. He fell away, lost his balance, and tumbled down the first flight of stairs.

With his muttering over, it was quiet except for my panting. I wiped the sweat out of my eyes with my good hand. At the landing, I couldn't see him, only one of his fingers. It wasn't moving. I was terrified it would start up again. I was terrified it wouldn't.

I regained my footing so I could shove my hand back up, try to stop the pressure from the hatch.

How long would I have to stay like that? I hung my head and tried to regroup my strength and sanity.

"Eli?"

My head swung toward the voice. Lucas stood there in

his blue outfit. He was breathing hard and looking up at me. "What happened to . . . him?"

"He tried to stop me from going out. He hurt me."

Lucas frowned. "That was mean."

"Yes, yes, it was."

He climbed the stairs and stood beside me. "You shouldn't have put your hand in there."

"I know." I tried to remain patient, keep my tone level. "It was stupid. But I need you to help, okay?"

He nodded.

There wasn't enough time to send him all the way back down to get Lexie or Terese. Not with Dad lying there. I had an idea. "Do you think you can climb up my back?"

He looked me up and down. "I think so."

Although I was tethered to the hatch by my arm, I was able to bend one knee so he could get a foothold to clamber up to my shoulders.

"Thataway. Now, go on up to my neck."

He seemed hesitant.

"Lucas, you can lean right on that wall with one hand."

He was in place, his legs twisted around my shoulders. He hardly weighed anything. "Good job. Okay, here's what you need to do. Try and reach through the opening where my hand is. See if you can't push some of that away. Pull it in if you have to."

My face was tilted up to check his progress. I was rewarded with a clump of dirt right in my open mouth.

I spit it out. "You're doing great."

A few more minutes and he had freed my hand. I rubbed

the raw wrist. Nothing broken, but it still hurt like hell. I would deal with the pain later. Both of my hands went to hold his legs. I urged him to keep moving dirt. Finally he'd moved enough for me to get my hands through the opening. I set him down so I could work. But I got to a point where I couldn't reach any more dirt. The hatch was nowhere near open enough. At least not open enough for me.

I looked at him. "Lucas, do you think you can squeeze through there?"

"I think so."

"You might get a little more dirt on you."

His eyes widened. "Real dirt? Like where the worms in my book live?"

I laughed. He hadn't ever seen real dirt. Didn't realize that's what he'd been shoving aside for the last half hour. "This *is* real dirt." I picked some up from the floor, sifting it through my fingers.

He grinned.

I lifted him up on my shoulders.

"Here I go." He squeezed through the opening. I felt funny watching his little legs kick, then disappear from my view. Maybe I was feeling protective.

"Okay, Lucas. Now, can you kick all the dirt off the hatch?"

Silence.

"Lucas?"

His muffled voice was loaded with wonder. "Are these real stars?"

My hands clutched the edge of the hatch harder. I leaned

my head on the wall. It was nighttime. My voice quivered. "Yeah, buddy. Those are the real thing."

Kicking sounds started.

Shoving even harder, I needed to see the night for myself. I felt the hatch give way, creaking upward until it flopped over, lying flat.

My head emerged into the summery air, fresh and heavenly. I breathed deep. The breeze blew cool against my face.

Lucas stood there, looking up. His mouth was wide open.

I stepped all the way out. My eyes shifted upward, seeing what he saw.

The night sky seemed like it was there just for us. I'd forgotten how beautiful stars were. And the moon. It wasn't much more than a sliver. I knelt beside Lucas and pointed it out. He was seeing it all for the first time. It was like the first time for me as well. I stood, and took a few steps as I smiled up at the sky.

There were so many things I'd taken for granted. So many things I hadn't appreciated. So many things I'd missed. Too many to even comprehend. "There's so much for you to see. I can't wait to show you."

The light from the hatch went out.

I turned around. "Lucas?" The moon wasn't bright enough to light the night for me. "Lucas?" I reached out, took a step toward where he had last been. My foot brushed the edge of the hatch. I knelt down to touch it.

The hatch was closed. And I was on the outside.

CHAPTER TWENTY-ONE

"No!" On my knees, I pounded the metal with both fists. "Open it! You can't do this!" I yelled and pounded until I was hoarse and could take no more of the pain shooting up my arm. I sat on the hatch, cradling my wrist.

The night was quiet. Too quiet. Shouldn't there be search helicopters all over this place? If Eddy and Gram . . .

If.

That was the word.

What if . . .

Eddy and Gram were really gone? What if I'd been IM'ing Dad all the time? What if this was just some twisted game, some way to get me out of the hatch? Except he took the code back and truly didn't expect me to decipher it again. So that there was no chance of me going outside.

Then I gasped and really looked around. Except for the

night sky, which would still be there anyway, how did I know there hadn't been a nuclear war? Dad had admitted so many things, but he could have said anything, made it up. I wrapped my arms around my knees and sunk my head into them.

Why wouldn't he want me in there, after trying so hard to keep me from finding the way out? I was the only one who could match him, physically. Now that I had found my way out, was there something he had to do without me around? Something I would have stopped him from doing?

The night was chilly, and I wasn't dressed for it. After a while I got hungry, and I was thirsty, too. It was almost funny, in a way—longing so much to get out, then wishing to be back in.

A whipping sound got louder as a light came toward me from the sky. A helicopter. I was on my feet in one second, jumping up and down and waving my arms. "Here! Over here!" I started to run toward the light, and then realized I might never find the hatch again. So I stayed where I was.

The helicopter moved toward me and landed about fifty yards away. The dust whirled around me, getting in my eyes, my mouth. I covered my face with my hands, peering through my fingers.

As I waited, the propeller gradually slowed as the whining of the engine grew quiet. The night was silent again as the searchlights stayed on. Backlit by them, a figure strode toward me.

"Hey, over here!" I waved my arms again, even though it was obvious the person saw me.

A flashlight shown in my face as I started spilling everything. "I'm Eli Yanakakis, my family is down in the hatch, and we—"

"Man, you got pretty big down there."

The voice was familiar. I tried to shield my eyes from the flashlight.

Finally he turned the light on himself. Hair a bit grayer. Phil. Dad's accountant. And, evidently, erstwhile helicopter pilot.

My hand dropped to my side. "What the hell are you doing here?"

He shrugged. "Safety net. You know, your dad was panicked when he called me, he really didn't expect you to figure out that code."

I took a step back.

"So, I flew all the way out here to . . . rectify the situation."

I glared at Phil. "What are you going to do?"

He ignored me and leaned over the hatch. He rapped the flashlight on it three times. The hatch flipped open. Phil reached into it and helped my father, who stepped out into the night. Phil's jaw dropped when he saw Dad's face, already swollen and bloodied from where my foot had connected. Phil asked him if he was okay.

Dad nodded, even though his walk was a little unsteady as he gazed up at the starry sky, just as I had done. He took a few deep breaths and half-smiled, half-winced. "I think it's time we moved this operation aboveground for a while."

Phil laughed. "Above or below, you still make more money than anyone on the planet."

Dad reached over and gripped Phil's shoulder. "Good to see you."

Phil leaned his head toward me. "He didn't get into too much trouble out here. Everything set in there?"

Dad nodded. "We just need to get my family and we'll be ready to go."

"Go?" I looked from Dad to Phil. "Go where?"

Dad spit some blood into the dirt and focused on me. "I think it's time we all got some sunshine. Remember that South Pacific island I bought when you were younger? Phil here has been building us a very nice place. Where we can be a family."

"I'm not going!"

Dad scratched his neck. "So what are you going to do? Run?" He spread his arms out wide. "There's nowhere to go."

I looked on either side of me, as far as I could see. Nothing. I could outrun both of them, I knew it. But it wouldn't change the fact that no matter what I did, my mother and my brothers and my sisters down below were still in the hands of my father. If I ran, and even if I found help, I might lose my family forever.

Phil chuckled at my distress. I realized at that moment he could have arranged for our food supply to be replenished, if only Dad had asked him. If only.

Phil turned to Dad. "You really don't look so good. Have any trouble with those charges?"

Dad shook his head as, with a slightly shaky hand, he handed a small black box to Phil.

"What charges?" I looked from Dad to Phil. "What did you do?"

Phil held up the box. "Once we're airborne, I simply flip the switch. There's enough explosives down there to turn this place to dust. And then you're off to a new compound in the South Seas."

My hands curled into fists. "I'm not trading this prison for a new one."

Phil started to climb down the hatch. "You don't really have a choice."

He concentrated on the stairs, so much so that he didn't see me coming, and I hit him broadside, knocking him down that first set. His body cushioned my fall, and the remote flew out of his hand as I got him in a choke hold.

His body stiffened as a loud, pulsing beep sounded from the Compound.

I let him go as my hands went over my ears.

Phil screamed several choice words and then poked a finger in my chest. "Stupid kid! You set it off!" He scrambled to his feet and climbed back out of the hatch to where Dad was leaning over, looking down at us.

Dad shouted over the blaring of the alarm. "How much time do we have?"

Phil held out his hands. "The warning only sounds in the last ten minutes!" He grabbed Dad by the arm. "Let's get out of here, Rex!"

"No!" Dad yelled back. "I have to get them out!"

Phil held up a hand. "I'm starting the chopper! And I leave in nine minutes, with or without—"

Dad clutched Phil's collar, the veins in his arm bulging with the strength of the grip. His voice was a roar, even over the alarm. "You'll leave when I say so!"

And then I turned and ran, as fast as I could, throwing myself down the stairs, trying to jump down whole flights as the warning signal blared raucously all around me. I had no idea how long I truly had. I hoped Dad would help, but I couldn't wait for him.

My first stop was the yellow room, and I slammed into the door with my shoulder. The dresser was still in place, so I could only reach through with my arm.

"It's me! Open the door!"

The little ones were crying, as Terese and Lexie tried to reassure them. Lexie stood up. "What's that sound?"

"Help me move this!" I could barely breathe enough to speak.

I shoved as Lexie pushed, and we got the dresser out of the way so the door could open. I was still panting. "Get out! You've got to go." I pointed at Lucas until I could get more words out. "He knows the way. Lucas, take them outside, up the hatch and out. Then run as far away as you can."

Terese started to say something, but I shouted, "Go! This place is going to explode!" Not waiting to make sure they complied, I headed for the infirmary at a sprint.

I turned down the hall and nearly collided with my

mother as she staggered down the hallway, clutching her stomach with one hand and covering an ear with the other. There were bloodstains on her nightgown. "What's going on?"

"Dad wired the place to explode, we've got to go!"

Her eyes widened as she yelled, "Where are the children?"

"On their way out!" I moved to pick her up.

She tried to shove me away. "Leave me!" She motioned toward the direction of the yellow room. "Get them out!"

"Mom—they're ahead of us already!" With one arm around her and the other under her legs, I lifted her, just as Dad rounded the corner.

He stopped, trying to catch his breath. He put one hand on the wall, and looked at my mother.

"Rex?" Mom reached out a hand to him. "What have you done?"

He didn't answer, but stood up straight and started to push by me.

"Dad! I need your help to get everyone out."

Hesitating, he looked one more time at my mom. "I need to get my research!" And he continued down the hall.

I paused.

Mom yelled in my ear, "GO!"

There was no time to waste, and as we headed for the exit I felt stupid for thinking he would actually help. Mom tried to put her arms around my neck as I jolted her along. I had no strength left as I started up the stairs, jogging them as fast as possible, praying the others were already out.

My pace was not one I could sustain for long, and I had to stop several times on the way up to catch my breath. Mom's arms tightened around my neck each time I stopped, and I understood it meant we needed to hurry.

At the hatch I had to stop and gather my strength for the last push up and out. The warning signal got faster then, and I shoved Mom out, followed her, then picked her up again and began to run in the night, away from the helicopter. If Phil wanted us, he'd have to work for it.

My lungs felt as if they would burst, and my arms and legs burned as I just kept running. For all I knew, it wouldn't be enough. I might be running right over the Compound. Then a series of quakes ruptured under my feet, a huge one rippling the ground beneath me, pitching us forward. Several other blasts in succession sent trembles under me. And then the ground was still.

My mother lay a few feet away from me. I crawled to her. "Mom?"

She moaned.

At least she was still alive.

I heard the whirring of the helicopter as it lifted off. It was nearly three hundred yards away and quickly disappeared from view. Was Dad on it? I was quite certain Phil didn't have the nerve to leave without him.

Silence.

"Lexie!" I yelled. When I got no answer, I began to scream, "Lexie! Terese!" I screamed their names in every direction before stopping and putting my head in my hands. "Oh my God, what did I do? I should have made sure . . ." I started to sob.

And then I realized maybe they were on the helicopter with Dad and Phil.

Would that be the worst thing? I turned around the way I'd come, where an acrid smell drifted toward me. My brothers and sisters being on the helicopter, safe, would not be the worst thing.

Mom was silent, but I felt her throat and found a strong pulse. I rolled her on her side so she could breathe easier. My sigh was loud in the night, and as my lungs filled with fresh air I wanted to just keep breathing in more and more. She moaned a bit, but didn't wake up.

Would it just be the two of us from now on? Or was it just a matter of time before more helicopters showed up to take us away?

I lay down on my back beside her on the dusty ground and stared up at the sky. A satellite went slowly across. That had to be a good sign, if the satellites were still there.

And as I listened to the nothing of the night, a faint scream bit into the silence.

I sat up.

The scream got louder.

I jumped to my feet.

And then it became a shout. "Eli!"

Out of the dark to my left, becoming more visible as they neared, was the rest of my family. Lexie carried the two little ones and Terese held Lucas.

I ran to them, enveloping Lexie and Terese in my arms, getting the rest of them at the same time. My face smashed in Lexie's shoulder, my words were a mumble. "I thought you all were gone."

Terese admonished me. "You said run. You didn't say which way."

Lexie was breathing hard as she set the little ones down. She shook out her arms. "We saw the helicopter and ran the other way."

Terese put Lucas down and pointed at Lexie. "She made us keep running and running. I thought we were lost."

I had to smile.

Lexie lowered her voice. "Where's Dad?"

I shrugged, then shuddered. "Either the helicopter or . . ."

She looked in the direction of the hatch. "Did it blow?"

"You didn't feel it?"

She shook her head. "We smelled it, though."

I took a deep breath, hoping it would clear my head. "We need to take care of Mom."

Lexie clutched my arm. "And then what do we do?"

"We wait." I grabbed a hand of each of the little ones, while Lexie and Terese each took one of Lucas's hands. Once we reached Mom, I plopped down beside her and spread out my legs, trapping Quinn between them. He leaned back into me and pointed skyward. "Pitty. Pitty."

I looked up at the stars. "Yeah, they are pretty."

Within moments, the sky grew lighter in the east, and I could see everyone more clearly.

Mom still seemed to be resting okay. Her hair had drifted around her face and she looked peaceful.

Lucas found a stick and drew in the dirt, humming as he worked.

Cara took handfuls of dirt and screeched as she threw them up into the breeze.

Terese held her arms out to her sides and spun and spun and spun, until she got so dizzy she fell, giggling, to the ground.

Lexie undid her braid, spread her hair out on her shoulders, and stood, eyes closed, as the wind softly blew her long hair out behind her.

I saw a couple of lights in the still dark sky to the west. As they neared, I started to hear them. On my feet at once, I said, "Helicopters."

Lexie came to my side.

Terese stood on my other side and leaned into me, linking her arm in mine. She was shaking. "Are they good or bad?"

I put an arm around her. "We'll have to wait and see."

The choppers landed about a hundred yards away. The dust rose in swirls around them. One was very big and nearly a dozen people got out. Several wore flak jackets and carried weapons.

I nudged Lexie. "Get the little ones."

They were just a few feet away, and she quickly hustled them over to where we stood.

Other men got out of the helicopter and started our way.

I took a few steps in front of my family, arms out to my sides. "Stay behind me."

Through the haze of dust, we saw someone leap out of the helicopter. Someone not in uniform. There were shouts, and one of the uniformed men grabbed him immediately, trying to restrain him, but his arms and legs thrashed, and he broke free, running in our direction, the others giving chase.

But they couldn't catch him. He would reach us before they did, and I had no way of knowing his intentions.

My stance became wider, firmer.

But as he got closer, I saw he was me. With longer hair.

My arms wavered where I held them.

But he couldn't be me. Because he was screaming my name, long and drawn out, almost mournful.

He sprinted closer, arms pumping, legs nearly a blur, and I began to tremble.

When he got within twenty yards, he started to slow, until he was jogging, and then he was walking.

He was there, in front of me, and halted only a step away.

From behind me, in reverent tones, Terese and Lexie spoke his name.

My shaking arms dropped of their own accord. I stepped forward to close the gap between us and found myself wrapped in a tight embrace.

An embrace that smelled blessedly familiar of jerky, smoky and greasy.

Eddy.

My breaths became sobs that matched his, shudder for shudder.

We were saved.

EPILOGUE

THE FIRST RAYS OF MORNING SUN CREEP TOWARD ME AS I straddle my surfboard in the warm Hawaiian waves. Except for the waterproof brace on my wrist, I assume I'm indistinguishable from any of the other early-morning surfers bobbing near me. For all intents and purposes, I could be one of the locals, deeply tanned and taking advantage of the superb dawn wave action. Nothing on the outside gives any indication of where I've been and what I've seen.

The rescue is becoming a blur. I had been operating on adrenaline, and reuniting with Eddy had shut everything down, made me a basket case. But I do remember, quite clearly, parts of that night.

The FBI and National Guardsmen threw those shiny silver blankets over each of us and hustled us onto one of the helicopters. They wanted to take Mom straight to the hospital on the medevac chopper, but she refused to be separated from us. And we made our intentions just as clear not to be apart from her. So they flew us to our cabin, where they had set up a base of operations after Gram had called them about the IM conversation. Phil's helicopter had led them right to us. On the ride, Mom clung to Eddy and cried, before releasing him long enough for him to meet his new siblings. He was surprised, but didn't stop grinning for a second.

When we reached the cabin, the place was swarming with people in uniform. We stepped off the helicopter and I heard a bark.

Cocoa.

I leaned down, my arms embracing her as she leaped into me. Cocoa's cold nose went straight into my neck.

"Hey, girl."

In my ear were those little pig-like grunts she'd always made. Her tongue was warm and wet on my face, licking at the tears that were rolling freely again. I laughed, trying to push her down even as I petted her. She was a little gray around the muzzle, but still smelled like cedar chips and dog shampoo.

Then Gram was there. I waited my turn. As she came to me, sobbing and moaning, my mouth crumpled and I wept yet again. We all did. Gram encircled me with her ample arms and smothered me with kisses that left me reeking of White Shoulders and Bengay. Nothing ever smelled so good to me.

Els stood behind her, tinier than I remembered. I towered over her by more than a foot. Naturally her expression was one of disapproval. But I was even relieved to see her.

With tears still running down my face, my arms went around her, picking her up off the ground.

She smacked me on the head with her purse. "You brat."

I set her down. Not before I noticed she had tears in her eyes. With one small, wrinkled hand she reached up to pat my face. "The house was too quiet. I haven't had a headache for six years."

I laughed and told her not to get used to it.

After our initial family reunion, a few members of the FBI pulled me aside for questioning. Of course, everyone thought Dad had been killed in an RV fire with the rest of us six years ago. Although the rest of us showing up alive shot some major holes in that story, and we had proof he'd been alive in the Compound: four more siblings. But we had no proof he wasn't dead now. Because we actually didn't know ourselves.

Medical personnel flew Mom to the hospital in Spokane where she had our little brother, Finnegan. We were all reunited a couple days later at our house in Seattle. We flew on a private jet, and on the drive from the airport, I stared out the limo's privacy glass at the world I hadn't seen in so long.

I hadn't expected people to be flying in spaceships, but I was a little disappointed. Other than different makes and colors of cars, and new buildings everywhere, the changes were subtle. I didn't feel as alien as I'd expected. The world had gone on without us, but we hadn't been left behind.

The first week home was a nightmarish one of being

surrounded 24/7 by news vans topped with satellite dishes, and reporters doing the evening news. We kept the curtains shut and watched television, careful to stay away from any news channels. Which seemed to be every other channel. So we watched reality television. Like the people on the islands who had to survive on nothing and then got voted off. Funny, none of us really liked that one. Too big a dose of reality.

Phil did a few interviews, speaking officially for the company. He stated how emphatically joyful he was that we were all alive and how sad that Rex Yanakakis, brilliant founder of YK Industries, had not been found with us.

Lying dirtbag. He also took the opportunity to reiterate the intricacies of my father's will, read six years before upon his "death," which left control of the company to Phil until Eddy, the sole heir, turned twenty-five. I assumed that the rest of us turning up alive would put a few kinks in Phil's plan, but that would remain to be seen.

Of course, the media involved weren't all legitimate press. The tabloids had a field day with the available facts. One story had us abducted by aliens who kept us for six years, then let us all go except my dad. Some papers even took the angle that the rest of us had gone to live there without him and he'd been searching for us in the RV when he was killed. Crazy, what those rags came up with. And those were only the ones Els snuck into the house. Mom saw them and, despite still recovering from the ordeal, decided it was necessary to hold a press conference.

Dressed in a dark suit with her hair up, she looked

beautiful, serene, and strong as she stood right out in the driveway and made a statement. Basically she told them to believe what they wanted to, but she and her children had lives to lead. She conceded that she would allow Phil to run the company for now, but anticipated that she and her two oldest sons would soon be major players in the world of YK Industries. She then stated the family would be taking an extended vacation, and alluded to us leaving for the Colorado house in a few days, where she graciously but firmly stated that she hoped the press would leave us alone.

And one of the private YK Industries jets did leave for Colorado that evening, but none of us were on it. We were on a chartered jet bound for the Big Island and Gram's house. Luckily, through all the chaos, no pictures of us ever emerged, so people weren't recognizing us on the street. We'd all changed too much. Gram had kept Eddy sheltered all those years, so his face, and mine, managed to be relatively anonymous as well.

Every passing day in the sunshine and salt water slightly dulls the fear. I don't know if there's enough blue sky or waves in the world to push me toward anything resembling forgiveness, let alone a feeling of security. But we plan to stay as long as the respite lasts. I suppose something will intrude eventually. Perhaps Phil? The company? The world?

Or perhaps my father.

A set of waves comes, and I ride the third nearly all the way before it bucks me, spilling me off my board and into the water. My head bursts above the water and I gasp in air. I grab my board, climb on, and paddle back out to try again.

⊛

Eddy and I spend a lot of time these days playing with the little kids on the beach, watching Cocoa chase Lucas and Cara in and out of the waves as Quinn sits in the sand, throwing handfuls into the air and screeching.

And we find ourselves teaching them about the world. Small stuff, dumb stuff we would never even think needs to be taught. Like the postal service. Fire sirens. Litter. Lucas has appointed himself the official litter patrol, as every day at the beach, at least once, he'll yell out "Litter!" before chasing after whatever happens to be blowing along the sand.

Eddy wondered why I didn't know the little ones that well, and he was silent as I told him the reason. He doesn't seem to judge any of us.

Another set of waves comes, but I stay where I am, letting them push me up before they slide on by.

Lexie and Terese spend most days with Gram's horses. I think the animals provide something the rest of us can't, but Lexie laughs easily now and then, and Terese hasn't gone back to an English accent.

Life is okay. Good, actually.

The sun comes up farther, and the beach is awash with sun. A group of people, burdened by coolers and beach towels and sun umbrellas, slowly trudges onto the beach. The tallest one turns my way, drops his load, and waves both arms.

I ride the next wave in, then tuck my board under my arm and jog toward them.

Lucas waves, then frowns and points behind me. "Litter!"

I motion for him to stay where he is, and reply, "I'll get it."

Grinning at his obsession, I turn and notice a small bit of white in the sand a few steps behind me. I bend over, pick it up, and take a quick glance.

My grin fades as I take a closer look.

A Tums wrapper.

More accurately, a half-empty roll, which was why it hadn't blown away.

I shade my eyes and look behind me into the rising sun, where the stretch of beach is empty. Then I look back toward the others, where they are setting up, ready to enjoy another day of their new lives.

With a shaking hand, I stuff the Tums in my pocket and hurry to join my family.

ACKNOWLEDGMENTS

This novel would not exist without the combined actions of the following:

My champion agent, Scott Mendel, and his astute comments on draft after draft as he waited for me to find the story. My fairy godmother of an editor, Liz Szabla, and her brilliant guidance as I traversed a new genre. My stalwart e-mail buddy, Sarah Van Dyke, and her bottomless support throughout the entire roller-coaster creation of this book. My forthright daughter, Bailey, for asking me, "This is really good, are you sure *you* wrote it?" My tenacious daughter, Tanzie, and her daily reminders that I am a mother who writes, not the other way around. My husband-of-the-year, Tim, and his patience with my incessant musings about plot and character. Those ingenious folks at NaNoWriMo and the annual opportunity they give all of us wannabe novelists a chance to prove we have it in us.

For everyone above, and all the other friends, family, and first readers who helped lead me to the end result, my Grandma Stuve would have said it best:

Thank you much.

DANGER

Thank you for reading this **FEIWEL AND FRIENDS** book.

The Friends who made

THE COMPOUND

possible are:

Jean Feiwel, **PUBLISHER**

Liz Szabla, **EDITOR-IN-CHIEF**

Rich Deas, **CREATIVE DIRECTOR**

Elizabeth Fithian, **MARKETING DIRECTOR**

Elizabeth Usuriello, **ASSISTANT TO THE PUBLISHER**

Dave Barrett, **MANAGING EDITOR**

Nicole Liebowitz Moulaison, **PRODUCTION MANAGER**

Jessica Tedder, **ASSOCIATE EDITOR**

Allison Remcheck, **EDITORIAL ASSISTANT**

Ksenia Winnicki, **MARKETING ASSISTANT**

Find out more about our authors and artists and our future publishing at www.feiwelandfriends.com.

OUR BOOKS ARE FRIENDS FOR LIFE